Home Is Where the Heart Is

WELCOME TO REDEMPTION, BOOK 5

DONNA MARIE ROGERS

ISBN: 978-1-941829-09-7
Published by Donna Kowalczyk
Contact Information: www.DonnaMarieRogers.com

Cover Design: The Killion Group, Inc.
Interior Formatting: Author E.M.S.

Published in the United States of America.

To the GGBA,
some of the best friends a writer could have.

Barbara Raffin. Your support and
keen GMC sense have been invaluable—Thank you.

Praise for Donna Marie Rogers

THAT MAGIC TOUCH
"Sheer genius. I will now put all future books by this author on my must read list."
—5 Stars, Amazon Reviewer

THERE'S ONLY BEEN YOU
"Love lost and found is the basis of this wonderfully heartwarming read. Throw in a years-old lie and a strong sense of family and it only gets better and better."
—4 Stars, RT Book Reviews

"Readers of contemporary romance will be thoroughly delighted...Donna Marie Rogers delivers a tender tale of love, family, and second chances."
—5 Bookmarks, Wild on Books

MEANT TO BE
"The plot kept me spellbound throughout the entire book. Rogers has the ability to keep her readers on the edge of our seats."
—5 Hearts, The Romance Studio

"The material is tightly written, well plotted and fast paced, and the characters are unforgettable."
—5 Books, Long and Short Reviews

WELCOME TO REDEMPTION SERIES
"With their easy, breezy style and skilled characterizations, Rogers and Netzel have created a town that readers won't want to leave."
—4½ Stars – RT Book Reviews

Donna Marie Rogers' Titles

LAKE SHELBYVILLE SERIES
That Magic Touch

JAMISON FAMILY SERIES
There's Only Been You
Foolish Pride
Meant To Be

DOUBLE M RANCH SERIES
Golden Opportunity
Golden Dream

WELCOME TO REDEMPTION SERIES
(small town romance series with Stacey Joy Netzel)
A Fair of the Heart (Book 1)
The Perfect Blend (Book 3)
Home Is Where the Heart Is (Book 5)
Never Let Me Go (Book 7)
Say You Love Me (Book 9)

Chapter One

"You know, Bianca, I never thought I'd admit this to anyone, but I'm sort of glad to be back." Lindy Spalding exited the highway and turned left onto Salvation Avenue. "I know it doesn't look like much at first. Charming in a gag-me-with-a-spoon sort of way. But I have to confess, I haven't been able to get the place out of my mind." She rolled up to a stoplight and cast her snoozing passenger a quick glance. "Come on, sleepyhead, I'd like you to see this. The snowfall really is quite spectacular."

Bianca's eyelids finally lifted, and those big baby blues glanced out the window with disdainful boredom. Her nose crinkled as if she smelled something foul. Lindy couldn't help but laugh.

"I know, believe me. That fresh air is hard to get used to. But you'll adjust."

Lindy drove slowly down the snow-covered road, a reluctant smile settling on her face as she passed *Coffee To Chai For*, the shop owned by her brother, Matt, and his girlfriend, Carrie. Her smile faded as she neared D.P. Tire & Auto. Half expecting to see that freight train of a dog race out in front of her, as it had on her first visit to the tiny Wisconsin town, Lindy breathed a sigh of relief when she made it past without incident. Even if a tiny part of her had hoped to catch a glimpse of its 'too-hot-for-his-own-good' owner, Drew Porter.

"You're an idiot, Melinda," she muttered to herself. With any luck she'd be able to avoid the big bully until she headed home in spring.

For some inane reason, the thought of leaving again when she hadn't even officially arrived back brought an ache to her chest. She had mixed feelings about Redemption—part of her wanted to stay, part of her thought she was nuts for even thinking it. Frustrating, to say the least.

Feeling a pair of hostile feline eyes on her, Lindy cast her grumpy passenger a sidelong glance. "Now don't you look at me like that. I told you we'd be here for a few months; it's not like you didn't have advance warning." She let out a heartfelt sigh. "Look, you know I'm only doing this because Daddy guilted me into it. But I promise, as soon as I get the plant in order, it's back to L.A. and civilization."

And daydreaming about a certain auto mechanic with the most incredible ocean blue eyes she'd ever seen.

Following Salvation Avenue as it curved left and led into Wyndhurst—the oldest section of town according to Matt—Lindy snatched her MapQuest directions off the seat and tried to read them without taking her eyes off the slick road. Just her luck the rental company hadn't had a single car with a GPS system. She knew to watch for an old abandoned church on the left, then the town's cemetery a mile or so past the church. The house she'd purchased to live in while in Redemption should be about three miles north of the cemetery on the right. Lindy tossed the MapQuest print-out back on the seat and glanced at her odometer.

As she crested a hill, a colossal white Victorian seemed to rise up out of the earth, majestic and beautiful, like something Norman Rockwell would have painted. Lindy stared in awe as she drove closer and the charming house came into view.

Much bigger than she'd expected, it sat in the center of a huge, snow-covered lot surrounded by trees. A thick stand of tall pines lined the far side of the house, while several deciduous trees peppered the front yard. Such a sight her new home made. Breathtaking was the only word to describe it. Watching the swirling snow drift down, Lindy felt a pang of some indefinable emotion.

Lord, she hadn't even stepped out of her car, and already she was going soft.

Damned Mayberry.

Matt's Jeep and a black Dodge Ram sat in the driveway. Giving herself a mental shake, Lindy pulled in behind them and killed the engine. Keys and purse in hand, she opened the door of her dark gray Cadillac DTS rental car and stepped out onto the slick road, being careful not to let her white, calf-length leather coat touch anything. The temperature was holding steady in the low thirties, so the snow was rather slushy, and she cringed at the thought of having to toss her brand new white eel skin boots.

A quick glance at her watch confirmed she'd made great time from the airport. Not quite two-thirty; the sun shouldn't set for a few hours yet. Plenty of time to get settled, then head back into town for dinner and some shopping. Since she'd arrived nearly two weeks early, she doubted Matt had had a chance to stock the house with any food or necessities.

"Okay, girl, time to go check out our new home." Lindy reached inside to press the button for the trunk, then plucked Bianca from her pet carrier. The sassy feline meowed another grievance over her new lot in life, but allowed herself to be cuddled against Lindy's chest. "Don't worry, we'll be in a nice, warm house soon, and I promise, the first thing I'm going to do is dig you out a can of food."

Bianca gave Lindy's chin a lick, mollified for the time being.

Lindy held tight to Bianca as she carefully made her way to the back of the car, doing her best not to step in the muddy slush. All she really needed was her small Louis Vuitton, which held her toiletries and Bianca's food and dishes. She plucked it out, closed the trunk, and started for the stone path still visible through the thin layer of snow.

A loud "W*oof!*" split the silence. Lindy's head shot up just as a suspiciously familiar beast leapt off the porch and raced straight for her, big pink tongue lolling out of its mouth.

"Bo, get your ass back here right now!"

Lindy saw Matt jump off the porch in hot pursuit, then everything happened in warp speed. Bianca went wild trying to claw out of Lindy's arms, then broke free with a loud squeal a split second before Bo went airborne straight at Lindy, hitting her square in the chest and knocking her back into the snow. The big ox sneezed in her face, then scrambled to his feet and barked his fool head off before running after Bianca.

Stupid dog! Lindy tried to take a breath, but couldn't draw air into her lungs, and sat up in a panic.

Matt dropped to his knees beside her. "Try to relax. You just had the wind knocked out of you."

Seconds after he said it, she was able to draw in a huge lungful of cold, crisp air. Matt started to help her to her feet when someone ran up and grasped her other arm.

"I'm really sorry about that. Are you all right?"

Drew Porter.

He wore a red flannel shirt with a white T-shirt beneath, and a well-worn pair of jeans. His slightly mussed, sinfully dark hair brushed his collar, and those 'take me now' blue eyes gazed at her with concern. Lindy thought him to be about the sexiest sight she'd ever seen.

Oh, boy, not a good sign.

She pulled her mental safety cloak around her and gave an angry swipe to the front of her coat, dislodging his hands. "Peachy, *Lou*," she groused, calling him by the wrong name just to annoy him—as she had the last time they'd met. "Your mongrel of a dog just ruined my brand new, fifteen hundred dollar leather jacket."

Biting the inside of his cheek to keep from laughing, Drew managed to drag his eyes up from the two very large muddy paw prints stamped on her chest. Her lusciously ample chest. Man, did that dog have great aim. And great taste. Melinda Spalding was even prettier than he remembered, if that was possible. Her shiny blonde hair flowed well past her shoulders and those gorgeous eyes, whiskey brown and hypnotic, had kept him lying awake at night on more than one occasion over the past six months.

He recalled their first meeting last summer when she'd skidded into town in her expensive sports car and nearly turned Bo into roadkill. Okay, to be fair Bo had darted out in front of her and caused her to swerve. Didn't mean she'd had to scream at him like a banshee— even if she had been breathtaking in her fury.

"It's Drew. And I'll pay for the thing, just send me the bill. Christ, who spends fifteen hundred dollars on a jacket anyway? You could feed a family for months on fifteen hundred dollars." Seriously, the crap rich people wasted their money on was beyond him.

Her eyes narrowed. "Keep your money. I wouldn't want you to have to sell your truck to pay me. By the way, Spalding contributes annually to more than thirty charities, so you can keep your snide comments to yourself as well." She swung back to glare at Matt. "What the hell is he doing here anyway?"

Matt gave Lindy a hug and grinned at Drew over her shoulder—the shit.

Wrapping an arm around her, Matt explained, "Drew's been helping Caleb and me get the house ready for your arrival. Which, I might remind you, was supposed to be the week after next. Any particular reason you're so early?"

She cast Drew a quick glance, which he found rather interesting. "I think it's pretty obvious," he teased. "She missed me. Ain't that right, Hot Stuff?"

"Yeah, like a cold sore." Lindy stepped around him and snatched her bag out of the snow, cleaning it off with quick, furious swipes. Instead of answering Matt's question, she veered off in the direction Bo and her cat had headed. "Bianca! Come on, baby, it's freezing out here. Mommy wants to get inside."

Mommy? Drew shook his head, but kept his mouth shut.

They all stared in open-mouthed shock when the Great Dane appeared from around the side of the house carrying a very docile white fluff ball in his mouth by the scruff of its neck.

Lindy let out a yelp of outrage and turned to glare at him. "Aren't you going to do something? That beast you call a dog is slobbering all over my precious baby!"

"He won't hurt the thing, don't worry."

She looked so indignant it was a wonder her eyes didn't cross. "That 'thing' is a purebred Persian."

Bo released the cat, and it immediately started rubbing against his front legs, purring as loudly as a souped up Charger.

Drew winked at Matt. "Bo's got a way with the ladies."

"Too bad his master doesn't." Lindy turned to meet his gaze, hers holding a hint of challenge.

Nothing Drew liked better than a challenge. "If I want a woman badly enough, I get her. That you can count on." He dismissed her and looked to Matt. "Come on, I'll help you bring her bags in."

Muttering under her breath, Hot Stuff hooked her fancy bag over her shoulder, scooped up her cat, and marched through the snow toward the house.

Drew gave his head a shake as he eyed the amount of luggage in the trunk. The very spacious trunk. By the time he and Matt had it unloaded, Drew counted fourteen pieces—not including the one she'd carried in herself: six large suitcases, three small, two duffle bags, and three hanging suit bags. It took them two trips to get everything inside, and since the master bedroom—which she'd had remodeled with a Jacuzzi tub and a skylight above it—was on the third floor, it was two very long trips.

Matt gave him a thump on the back. "Thanks, man, I appreciate it. And I owe you dinner. Nino's sound good? I've got a taste for one of their beef sandwiches."

"Wish I could, but I have to pick Hannah up from work. Her car blew a tie rod, so I'm gonna work on it tonight. Raincheck?"

"You got it."

The differences between brother and sister never failed to surprise Drew. Both were heirs to an extremely vast fortune—their father the sole owner of Spalding Enterprises, one of the oldest and richest family owned companies in America. Yet Matt was as down-to-earth and friendly as Lindy was spoiled and pretentious.

Lindy joined them in the massive, two-story foyer. She held her jacket in the crook of her arm and had pulled that long, shiny hair up into a ponytail, baring her creamy throat. A skin-tight pair of jeans, no doubt designer, was tucked into those sexy high-heeled boots, and a low-cut, white cashmere sweater stretched taut over her full breasts. But what held his attention was the delicate gold chain she wore, its crystal pendant nestled in her generous cleavage.

Lucky stone.

She strolled up to Matt keeping her back to Drew. "I have to run into town for groceries, and I'll probably stop for something to eat as well. Oh, and I need to buy a couple of pillows for my bed. What time is that little department store open until today?"

Matt shot Drew an 'oh, shit' look. "Pretty sure they stay open 'til ten on Saturday. But you'll also need to buy a sleeping bag since you don't have a bed."

"Wha-at?"

Her voice had raised an octave, and Drew choked down another chuckle.

"Last time we spoke you said the painting was done and all the furniture had come in."

"No, I said all the *downstairs* furniture had come in. I delayed the delivery of all the bedroom furniture since you decided you wanted the rooms re-carpeted. You should have a bed by Friday."

Drew cleared his throat. "You know, Princess, if you can't handle sleeping on the floor for a few nights, the Rykers Inn ain't far from here."

That got her dander up. Lindy spun around and cocked her head in that haughty way that made him want to toss her over his knee. "The word is 'isn't', genius. And I'll be perfectly fine on the floor, thank you very much." She turned back to face Matt, effectively dismissing him.

Drew couldn't help but grin at her spunkiness.

Matt grinned as well.

"I should only be gone a couple of hours. Will you still be here when I get back?"

"Yeah, I'll be here. Caleb, too. He left a little while ago to pick up Max from his guitar lessons, run him home, then stop at the hardware store. We'd planned to get the last few ceiling fans put up today and hang a couple new doors on the second floor."

She turned slightly as she tucked a lock of hair behind her ear; her pursed lips softened into a smile. "Thank you, Matty. And please thank Caleb for me as well. In fact, he deserves a huge bonus. Hard to believe this is the same house you emailed me pictures of last October."

Drew silently agreed. The once magnificent old mansion had been transformed back to its former glory and then some after being nearly uninhabitable for years.

Matt glanced out the front window. "Looks like it's really starting to come down out there. Maybe you should wait until it dies down before heading into town."

"It's not supposed to die down until late tonight," Drew said. "We're expecting three to four inches, remember?"

"Hell, that's right, I forgot. In that case, it's probably best if you wait until tomorrow to do your shopping."

"Matt, I'll be fine." She smiled complacently. "It's not like I've never driven in snow before."

Before he had a chance to rethink the offer, Drew looked at Lindy. "Matt's right, you shouldn't risk it. Why don't you let me give you a lift into town? I have to pick my sister up from work, which happens to be the best diner in town. I could run her home while you eat, then come back and take you shopping." Christ, what was he, a glutton for punishment?

"No, thank you," she said without so much as a glance in Drew's direction. "Like I said, I'll be fine." Lindy shrugged into her muddied coat, dug out her keys, and strolled out the door.

Drew waited until he heard her engine turn over before muttering, "Your sister's a real charmer, Spalding."

Matt chuckled. "It's your own fault, man. You got under her skin."

"Lucky me." She'd gotten under his skin, too, though he'd die before admitting it. "I'd best get going. I'll see you tomorrow for the game, right?"

"You bet. Oh, and Carrie said to tell you she's bringing a big bowl of pretzel dip and a platter of deviled eggs."

"Tell her she's the best. See you later." Bo got up from the throw rug he'd been sleeping on by the fireplace and whined in the direction Bianca had taken off to before reluctantly following Drew outside.

The light snow had spiraled into a heavy downfall—virtually blizzard conditions. Lindy had just disappeared over the hill by the time he backed out of her driveway. He suspected Miss Snootypants had little experience driving in snowstorms, despite what she'd said, though that big Caddy should handle well enough in these conditions. Long as the driver knew what they were doing. Drew had some serious doubt on that score, but for Lindy's sake he hoped he was wrong.

As soon as he crested the hill he saw her car. Bo whined beside him, and Drew reached out to scratch him behind the ears. "Don't worry, boy, she'll be fine. Just to be safe, we'll follow her into town; make sure she arrives in one piece." Maybe he'd give Matt a call later, make sure she—

A deer shot out of the swirling white abyss right in front of the gray Caddy. Drew watched helplessly as Lindy swerved to avoid it and spun into a fishtail. She slid sideways a good fifty feet before winding up in the ditch on the opposite side of the road.

Drew pulled onto the shoulder and threw his door open, racing across the street as fast as the slushy snow would allow. Bo bounded out of the truck after him, beating him to the car. When Drew reached the driver's side of the Caddy, he tried to open her door, but it was locked. Lindy sat staring out the windshield, those big brown eyes round with shock.

He tapped on the glass, and she jumped before looking his way. He gestured for her to unlock the door. As soon as she did, Drew yanked it open and squatted down to get a good look at her. Bo stuck his head inside, but Drew pushed him back out of the way.

"You all right, Hot Stuff? You didn't hurt yourself, did you?"

She swallowed, finally took her hands off the steering wheel, and shook her head. "No, I-I'm fine. I just...I almost killed *Bambi.*"

Drew bit back a smile at her whispered pronouncement since she looked about ready to burst into tears. Interesting. She was more concerned about the deer than herself. His respect for her grew an inch. Maybe she wasn't quite as self-centered as she put on.

"The deer's fine, sweetheart, I promise. You didn't even come close. Now, why don't you let me drive you into town like I should've done in the first place?"

Surprisingly, she didn't argue. She merely grabbed her purse and climbed out, allowing him to lock up her car. She didn't even put up a fight when he swung her up into his arms and carried her to his truck. Bo ran ahead of them and jumped back inside.

So when Drew opened the passenger side door, she got a four-inch wide slobbering tongue across the face.

Chapter Two

"See boy, I told you she was all right. Bo was worried about you."

As soon as Drew set her on the seat, the mangy dog tried to lick her again. Lindy threw her hands up and wrinkled her nose in disgust. "I'm touched. Please tell me you have some wet naps in here...?"

"Sorry. You'll have to wait 'til we get to Hutch's." Whistling, he shut the door and walked around the front of the truck. When he got in on the driver's side, he pulled out his cell phone and made a call. "Hey, it's me. I need you and Tom to tow a car out of the ditch and drive it to the old Kendall place. Gray Caddy, new, a couple miles past the cemetery on

Salvation, right hand side of the road. And it's a rental, so be extra careful. Yep, thanks."

He disconnected and put the truck in gear. Lindy buckled her seat belt and held onto the door for dear life as the truck started forward, sliding a little here and there, but managing to stay on the road. The urge to close her eyes until they arrived at the diner was tempting, but the last thing she wanted to do was show this man anymore weakness than she already had.

Bo whined as he leaned over to sniff her ear, and then sneezed in her face for a second time.

"Eww!" She swiped at her face with her coat sleeve. "Come on, dog, that's just gross."

Drew chuckled and reached up to pat the monster's head. "Ease up on her, boy. The lady doesn't like dog snot on her. Most don't."

Bo whined again, reached his humongous paws onto the dash to stretch, then much to Lindy's amazement, he leaned into Drew's side and rested his big head on Drew's shoulder. Her heart softened just the teensiest bit toward both dog and master.

By the time Drew pulled into the parking lot of the diner, Lindy was in desperate need of some coffee. She opened the door and climbed out, grateful he'd thought to park under the overhang so she didn't have to step in ankle-deep wet snow. Drew cracked the window and instructed Bo to stay in the truck before escorting her inside.

As soon as he opened the door, a feast of delicious aromas pummeled her senses. "Mmm, it smells amazing in here." And much to her surprise, the place was fairly busy. *The food must be phenomenal for people to wander out in such weather*, she mused.

Drew led her to an open booth in the back. "I have a feeling Hutch is gonna ask Hannah to stay a little longer, so if you don't mind, looks like I'll be joining you for supper."

Lindy slid into the booth and dug her cell phone out of her purse. Okay, so she'd look like the biggest witch in the world if she said no considering all he'd done for her in the last twenty minutes. And since he couldn't possibly read her mind, the fact that his nearness brought on all sorts of fanciful thoughts would remain her own little secret. "That's fine. I'm going to give Matt a quick call so he doesn't worry when the tow truck pulls up with my car."

"Good idea. Be right back."

She hit the speed dial button for Matt, and then watched as Drew approached one of the two waitresses. He leaned down and exchanged a few words with her before heading into the rest room. Lindy hated that she couldn't seem to drag her eyes away from him.

When Matt answered his cell, she briefly explained what had happened and promised to do her shopping quickly. She'd just disconnected when Drew arrived back at the table, his sister right behind him. She set a couple of glasses of ice water on the table. Lindy immediately dunked a napkin in her glass and wiped the dog slobber from her face.

Drew sat down and made the introductions. "Hannah, I'd like you to meet Matt's sister, Lindy. Lindy, this is my baby sister, Hannah."

The young woman's smile was surprisingly shy. "Nice to meet you. I've heard a lot about you."

Oh, I'll just bet you have. "Nice to meet you, too, Hannah." What a beauty, Lindy thought, noting Hannah shared Drew's vivid blue eyes and near black hair. A stunning combination to be sure. The young woman looked to be maybe nineteen to twenty years old.

Drew drummed his fingers on the table as he perused the menu. "I'm in the mood for something different today. Think I'll try the hot beef plate, extra gravy, and a large root beer." He looked over at Lindy, a teasing glint in his eyes. "I suppose you want a salad?"

"Hutch makes a wonderful chicken caesar salad," Hannah suggested as she finished writing down Drew's order. She met Lindy's gaze and added, "But his cheeseburger and fries are the best in Wisconsin."

Lindy smiled, liking Hannah more by the minute. "Sold. I'd like my cheeseburger medium, with extra ketchup and no onions, please. Oh, and coffee."

Hannah's face lit up as she jotted down Lindy's order. "I'll be right back with your drinks."

Drew leaned back, his expression one of grudging respect. "Didn't think you had it in you to eat regular ol' diner food."

"What exactly is that supposed to mean?" She grabbed a napkin from the metal dispenser, swiped some of the condensation from her glass, and dabbed at her face.

He held up a hand in supplication. "Nothing, relax. I just didn't figure you for the cheeseburger type, that's all."

"And I didn't figure you for the type to use eating utensils, but unless you plan to suck your mashed potatoes through a straw, I guess I've misjudged you as well."

He leaned forward and lowered his voice. "You know what you need, Hot Stuff? A good, old-fashioned spanking. And if you don't watch that sexy mouth of yours, I'll pull you across my knee right here, right now."

"Are you threatening me?" she practically sputtered. Why of all the nerve! If he laid one hand on her, she'd—

"No threat, sweetheart, it's a promise."

He leaned back again, draping his arm across the top of the booth, his eyes slightly narrowed. Before she could summon up a reply, Hannah appeared and set their drinks in front of them, then headed back to the kitchen. Drew continued to eye Lindy in silent warning until Hannah returned with their plates. She pulled a bottle of ketchup from her pocket and set it on the table.

"Enjoy. If you need anything else, just let me know."

"Thank you, Hannah, it smells wonderful."

Silence stretched as they ate their food. Hannah had been right on the money, Lindy realized as she quickly devoured the best burger she'd ever eaten. She chanced a glance at Drew who had wolfed down his food with equal enthusiasm—or maybe he just couldn't wait to get away from her. The man frustrated her on so many levels it wasn't funny. She wanted to smack him; she wanted to wring his neck. And at certain weak moments she wanted to kiss him. The admission, even if only in her own mind, was enough to bring on a wicked case of heartburn.

Suddenly, a huge smile transformed Drew's face, and she craned her neck in time to see Matt's girlfriend, Carrie, enter the diner. She strolled up to the table and slid in next to Drew, who looked all too happy to see the buxom brunette. *Ass.*

Carrie cocked a brow at Drew, and then grinned at Lindy. "Matt called and asked me to come save you from Drew's evil influence."

"Hell, I'm the one in need of saving." He met Lindy's gaze, a mischievous twinkle in his eye. "She's mean to me, Care. I'm not sure my masculine pride can take much more."

"You're an idiot."

"See?"

Carrie chuckled. Lindy dug a fifty out of her wallet, tossed it on the table, and met Drew's teasing gaze. "Thanks for coming to my rescue."

His smile faded. He flipped the money back at her. "I don't need your charity, lady. I only did what anyone would've done."

"Fine, then the rest is a tip for Hannah."

"Hannah doesn't need your charity either."

24

Impossible man! "It's not charity, it's a tip. Waitresses earn tips; it's how they make the majority of their money."

"As if you would know anything about it."

Lindy shot to her feet and jammed her hands on her hips. "About what? Earning money? I'll have you know I work damn hard for my paycheck."

Drew gave a derisive snort. "Yeah, I'm sure filing your nails all day must get extremely tiresome. That and ordering some poor schmuck to fetch coffee must be worth, what—"

"Okay, I think that's enough." Carrie tweaked the hair at the nape of Drew's neck, earning a yelp, before sliding out of the booth. "Goodbye Drew. Lindy, Matt says you need to do a little shopping, so just tell me where you'd like to go."

Frustrated, Drew watched his longtime friend and the most infuriating woman he'd ever met stroll out the door. Carrie and Lindy couldn't be more different, yet Matt adored them both. And they seemed to get along fine...although Drew knew firsthand that wasn't always the case. Hot Stuff wasn't famous for making good first impressions.

Hannah approached the table with teasing trepidation. "Well, you still have your skin, I guess that's something."

"Funny." He pulled out his wallet and handed her a twenty, then nodded toward the fifty Lindy had left for her. "Miss Money Bags left you a tip."

"Cool." She snatched it up. "I'll have to remember to thank her."

"Sure, suck up to her. Money makes the world go 'round, right?"

Hannah frowned and plopped down across from him. "You've got it bad, big brother. Not that I blame you. Rich *and* beautiful. Not a bad combo by anyone's standards."

"Yeah, well you can get that idea out of your head right now. I like my women with a little less vinegar."

She let out an unladylike snort. "Please. You like women, *period*. And Miss Melinda Spalding is one very attractive woman."

Damn if that wasn't the truth. Though the snooty blonde was definitely more trouble than she was worth. "Can we change the subject, please?"

Hannah smirked, but her expression sobered as her eyes focused on something by the entrance. Drew followed the direction of her gaze and scowled when he recognized the cause of her distress—Jimmy Swan. "Thought you quit seeing that asshole."

"I did, but...he's having a little trouble letting go."

"Guarantee he'll get the message when I'm through with him." Drew shot to his feet and started forward.

Hannah grabbed his arm. "Drew, no! Please. Let me talk to him. I don't want to cause a scene, and I doubt Hutch would appreciate it, either."

Torn between wanting to put that loser in his place and not wanting to upset his sister, Drew dropped back down with a growl of frustration. He knew Hutch would understand if Drew pitched the bastard back out into the snow, but if Drew caused a scene he'd only succeed in embarrassing Hannah.

"Fine. But if he doesn't leave within five minutes, he's getting personally escorted out by my booted foot. Goddamn thief. I still think he snatched my autographed Donald Driver rookie card."

Drew watched in frustration as she headed over to speak with the little bastard. He never did understand what she saw in the guy. Jimmy Swan was short, lanky, and shifty-looking. Drew had been suspicious of him from the moment Hannah introduced them. But he'd only had his gut-instinct to go by and knew it wasn't fair to make snap judgments of people.

Unfortunately, he'd been right. The guy was a total loser. He couldn't keep a job, and he couldn't keep Mr. Happy in his pants. Drew only knew the latter because he'd found Hannah crying her heart out one night, curled up in the fetal position on the back porch swing. He'd wanted to kick Swan's ass into the next century for daring to disrespect his sister, but Hannah had begged him not to. His baby sister abhorred violence of any kind; she was the gentlest soul he knew. She'd forgiven the idiot twice for cheating on her, but this last time had been the final straw. Or so Drew hoped.

Jimmy finally left after giving her a peck on the forehead that would've looked sweet to anyone else. But Drew knew what a pig the guy was and could only pray someone more deserving of Hannah would come along soon.

"Come on, man, there has to be someone else in Redemption who owns a pickup—the Packers are playing in the Super Bowl! What about Caleb?"

In just a few hours, Drew would be hosting his annual Super Bowl party, and only the third in his lifetime featuring the Packers. The *last* thing he had time for was a trip into Green Bay for a mattress. Christ, what happened to, *"I'll be perfectly fine on the floor, thank you very much"?* Yeah, right, Princess.

"He's out on an emergency call, and Lauren isn't sure when he'll be back. Look, I know this is bad timing, but Carrie and Lauren are making most of the food anyway, and I can start grilling if you're not back in time."

The last thing Drew wanted to do was spend more time with Hot Stuff than he had to. She infuriated him like no woman ever had...she also excited him like no woman ever had, which was half the problem. Hell, who was he kidding, it was the majority of the problem. The urge to spank her warred with the need to kiss her breathless, and he knew he'd be a goner if he ever gave in to either urge.

"Fine, I'll do it. Tell her I'll be there in ten minutes."

"You're the best."

Drew could hear the humor in his friend's voice. "Yeah, well you're gonna owe me big time for this one."

"That I will. Thanks, man."

As soon as Drew pulled into Lindy's driveway, he regretted agreeing to play chauffeur. She stood on the porch with her arms crossed, her annoyance unmistakable. She dropped her arms and strode toward the truck, then stopped to glare at him through the windshield for a couple heartbeats before continuing on toward the passenger side door. Drew suddenly wished he'd brought Bo along to sit between them.

She yanked open the door and climbed in, slamming it closed with both hands. Drew was hard pressed not to laugh at her silent little tantrum.

"You're late."

He avoided her gaze as he backed out of the driveway. Damn, it was going to be a long ride into Green Bay. "Fifteen minutes. Get over it."

She buckled her seat belt and crossed her legs, one foot bouncing angrily as steam erupted from her ears. Thankfully, she ignored him for most of the ride, staring straight ahead while silently fuming. Finally, she started looking around at the scenery. A small smile even touched her lips.

"Pretty, ain't it?"

Her smile faded. It dawned on Drew that she was still angry with him from yesterday. So Hot

Stuff was a grudge holder. Perfect. He let out a long, drawn out sigh as he took the 41 exit south. "We'll be there in about ten minutes. Think you can handle my company that long?"

"If only it ended there," she muttered.

"Look, you don't like me, fine. I'll drop you off at the furniture store and you can take a taxi home. Maybe if you offer the driver enough money he'll strap your mattress to the roof of the cab."

At long last, she looked at him, and Drew was taken aback by the hurt glimmering in her eyes. "You think I'm just some useless fluff ball who doesn't do anything but file my nails and buy new clothes."

"Since when do you care what I think?"

She swung her gaze away and stared back out the windshield. "I don't."

Drew came up to a stoplight and took the opportunity to study her face. He reached out and cupped her chin. "Liar. I think you care more about my opinion than you want to admit."

She jerked her chin from his grasp and pinned him with her most haughty glare. He heaved a silent sigh. How nice it would be if she just quit this whole Paris Hilton act and joined him back on planet Earth. Little Miss

31

Silver Spoon was buried so deep in her privileged world he doubted it was possible to draw her out. And hell, who cared? She wasn't even worth the effort.

Now who's the liar, pal?

"Get over yourself, *Lou*, I couldn't care less what you think. You're nobody to me."

"You know damn well what my name is, lady, so say it. Call me by my name or you can take a taxi back to Redemption."

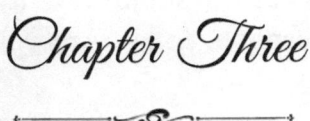

Chapter Three

$\mathcal{L}$indy's pulse quickened at the intensity in Drew's tone, of his stare, so in contrast with his normal carefree attitude. Although she could hardly blame him. She'd been acting the bitch since the moment he'd pulled into her driveway. And since the reason for her annoyance had more to do with her ungodly attraction to the man than anything he'd actually done, she supposed the least she could do was quit antagonizing him.

"Fine. *Drew.* Happy?"

A slow smile curved his lips. Those very nicely-shaped lips that looked oh-so soft and—

"Deliriously."

Lindy breathed a sigh of relief when they finally pulled into the parking lot of the furniture store.

Besides the mattress, she had several odds and ends she hoped to pick up today, so she planned to hustle through the store. A salesman approached as soon as they cleared the automatic doors. He couldn't have been any older than Hannah, but had that used car salesman smile down to a tee.

"Good afternoon, folks. Are you looking for something specific?"

"The lady needs a mattress. Can you lead us in the right direction?"

"I'd be happy to. Follow me."

He led them toward the left wing of the humongous store. Lindy stopped twice on the way; first for a polished brass lamp that would be perfect for her bedroom, and then a gorgeous small area rug that would look fabulous in front of the fireplace.

"Come on, Hot Stuff, I have a Super Bowl party to get home to."

"Relax, you have like three hours before the game starts. Even I can't take that long."

Two hours and forty-five minutes later, Drew and two store workers carried her new king-size mattress, box springs, and other items out to Drew's truck. Lindy tipped each man a twenty, but when she tried to give Drew some cash once they were seated inside, the ungrateful man growled at her.

"Keep your damn money. I just want to get home. As it is I'm gonna miss the first half hour of the game. *Even I can't take that long*," he mimicked, turning his key in the ignition.

"Well, you don't have to be so nasty. It's not like much happens in the first thirty minutes anyway. I mean, what? They prance out onto the field and slap each other's butts."

"Don't test me, lady," he advised, shooting her an evil glare. "I'll drop you off on the side of the road, and you can call a damn cab. Or better yet, your brother. I swear, I'm going to kick his sorry ass—"

"Don't you dare threaten Matt. This isn't his fault. I just...well, I tend to be choosy and—"

He snorted. "Now there's an understatement if I've ever heard one."

She crossed her arms and leaned back against the headrest. "Well, don't expect me to apologize for having discerning tastes."

"How 'bout apologizing for making me late to my own Super Bowl party? Think you can manage that?"

"I can't believe you're making such a big deal over this. I mean, it's not like I didn't try to pay you for your time."

Drew gave a disbelieving shake of his head. "You really think that's all that matters, don't you? Give the poor dumb schmuck a twenty dollar bill and he should grovel at your feet."

"I never said any such thing, nor do I think that way." Hurt and angry, she turned to face him. "Why are you being such a jerk? I'm sorry we're running late, but my God, you're acting as if I made you late to your own wedding or something."

"Can't you just say you're sorry and leave it at that?" he demanded. "As if a wedding was as important as the Super Bowl."

His ridiculously cavalier attitude toward marriage shouldn't have bothered her, yet it did. "No mystery why you're still single, is there?"

"I don't see a wedding band on your finger, either, Hot Stuff. And believe me, no mystery there, either." He pulled up to a stoplight and turned the full force of his irritation on her.

They eyeballed each other for several heartbeats, and then Lindy's breath caught as his gaze dropped to her lips. A car horn broke the spell and, with a muttered curse, Drew hit the gas and sped off.

Swirling, fat snowflakes started to drift down just as they turned off onto the highway that led back to Redemption. Lord, she couldn't wait to get home, get her bed set up, and soak in a hot tub with a good book. Dinner would be a nice roast beef sandwich and...Lindy sat up straight when Drew turned into his own driveway instead of heading on to her place.

"Why are we stopping? Aren't you taking me home?"

"Strong as I am, I can't carry a king-size mattress and box springs up two flights of stairs all by myself."

"Oh." Duh, she hadn't thought of that.

Drew climbed from the truck, and then met her gaze with an expectant lift of his brow. "Well?"

"Well what?"

"Don't you think it would be nice to come in and say hello?"

Lindy blew out a silent breath. While she liked all of Matt and Carrie's friends, she knew if she accompanied Drew inside, they'd be stuck there until the end of the game. And to be honest, Lindy would rather have a root canal than sit through an entire football game. Especially since her temples had started throbbing several miles back. Too bad she didn't have her laptop with her. She forced a smile. "Of course. Right behind you."

Squished into the corner of Drew's well-worn loveseat next to lovebirds Matt and Carrie, her ass wedged so far into the cushion they were going to need a crowbar to pry her out, Lindy wanted nothing more than to stick a fork into her temple and end her misery. She'd spent the last hour listening to a roomful of Mayberry's finest scream like banshees, causing her mild headache to morph into a full-blown migraine. My God, she hadn't thought it possible to dislike football any more than she already did, but holy touchdown she'd never been more wrong.

"Hey, Hot Stuff, want a hotdog?"

She glared up at the object of her misery with all the disgust and loathing she could muster considering her head was on the verge of implosion. "No. Thank you," she bit out, tempted to cram the proffered hotdog down his throat. "What I want is to go home, get my bed set up, and take a hot bath."

His smiled disappeared. "Can't you just relax and enjoy yourself for a change?"

"Once I'm submerged to my neck in bubbles, I'll relax and enjoy myself." She tried to stand, but the stupid couch sucked her back in. She shot him a look. "A little help, please?"

Drew shoved the hotdog into his mouth, at the same time he grasped her hand and plucked her from her cushiony hell. *Jackass.* She barely managed to keep her balance as he let go and stepped past her to give Matt's shin a kick.

"Hey, you ready to give me a hand with your sister's bed?"

"Now? Can't it wait till half-time?"

Drew gestured at Lindy with the hotdog. "Ask Princess Pain-in-the-Ass here."

"Drew, be nice," Carrie warned. To Matt, she said, "Go ahead, it's almost half-time anyway. If you hurry, you'll be back before the third quarter starts."

Matt gave Carrie a quick kiss. "Save my spot?"

She winked at him. "I'll even have Bo keep it warm for you."

Lindy rolled her eyes, but truthfully she envied them their comfortable relationship. Matt's happiness was important to her—and Carrie Lowell made him very happy indeed. For that reason alone Lindy had finally dropped her guard and welcomed the friendship Carrie offered.

Lindy said her goodbyes to the room in general, then preceded Matt and Drew from the house. Thankfully, Drew had thought to secure a tarp over her mattress and other items, as a layer of snow had accumulated. She knew she should thank him, but frankly, all she wanted to do was smack him upside the head.

The roads were slick, but they made it to her house without incident. Lindy held the door open as the men carried in her box springs and the mattress. They made quick work of it, too, bringing a reluctant smile to her face.

Matt helped her with the sheets while Drew ran back down to his truck for the lamp and area rug she'd purchased.

"I'll call tomorrow and see if I can get the rest of your furniture delivered earlier than planned."

Lindy stuffed a brand new pillow into its casing. "That would be great, Matty, thank you." She tossed the pillow on the bed and reached for the other. "So what do you guys have left to do in the house?"

"Not much. A few cabinets need to be replaced in the kitchen, and Caleb wants to build you a nice window seat in here." He met her gaze. "Not that you'll get much use out of it once the plant's up and running."

The same odd sadness that had tightened her chest yesterday returned full force, nearly stealing her breath. Dammit, she didn't want to become attached to this place—she wouldn't!

Giving herself a mental shake, Lindy broke eye contact and feigned absolute interest in the down comforter she'd managed to cram into her largest suitcase.

Matt reached out and grabbed an end to help her unfold it. "You do plan to visit, don't you?"

With a scoffing frown, she slid the comforter onto her bed, straightened it, and settled the pillows on top. "Suppose I'll have to if I want to see my favorite brother—who seems to have an aversion to the West Coast since settling into Mayberry."

Matt crossed his arms and pegged her with a considering look, as if he knew exactly why this town struck such fear in her. "I'm your only brother, and I've been to L.A. twice since last summer. Besides, you know better than anyone why I hate to go back there."

She did, and now she felt like a bitch for even bringing it up. "You're innocent of murdering that girl, Matty, and the whole world knows it. Besides, you've made a good life for yourself here in Wisconsin. And if you tell her I said this I'll deny it, but I think Carrie is the best thing that's happened to you. You're as fat and happy as I've ever seen you." Lindy cast him a cheeky grin.

Matt laughed and patted his belly. "I can't help it. Carrie loves to cook, and I'm her favorite guinea pig."

"I was teasing; you haven't put on a pound. Well, maybe a couple," she amended, grinning.

"But you've always been athletic. I'm sure as soon as the weather clears you'll get out there and run it off."

Drew's footsteps echoed up the stairs at a rapid rate. He strode into the room carrying her lamp, looked around, then walked over to the south facing window and set it on the sill. "All done, Hot Stuff. Enjoy your soak. Come on, Matt, let's go."

"See you tomorrow, Sis." Matt gave her a kiss on the cheek.

Feeling impish, Lindy asked Drew, "Can I give you a tip this time?"

He held her gaze for several heartbeats, and Lindy suddenly wished she hadn't poked the proverbial tiger.

"Matt, would you give us a minute, please?"

Lindy's heart tripped when Matt shrugged. He gave Drew a thump on the back, tossed her a smile, and whistled his way downstairs. Lindy bit the inside of her cheek as she lifted her gaze to meet Drew's. "I was only kidding, geez. I mean—"

Quick as a whip, Drew hauled her against the solid expanse of his chest and slanted his mouth across hers with near punishing force. Stunned, Lindy simply settled her hands against his chest. Then her senses returned, and she shoved with all her might. He broke off the kiss with a muttered curse, but didn't let her go. Lindy's pulse kicked into overdrive as she looked up and met his gaze.

Hypnotic blue eyes stared down at her, holding her gaze captive as if by physical force. Deft hands traveled a scorching path from the curve of her shoulders to the flare of her hips, leaving every inch of her body tingling in their wake. The need to feel his lips on hers again, to taste him, nearly overwhelmed her. A real kiss, though, not in anger, not as punishment. Before she lost her nerve, Lindy twined her arms around his neck and pulled him down for the real thing.

With a deep growl, Drew crushed her in his arms. He coaxed her mouth open as his tongue slid inside with skillful ease, exploring, seeking hers. Shivering under his touch, Lindy grew dizzy with yearning. Her heart thumped as his spicy masculine scent wrapped her in sensual bliss. The man was certainly no slouch in the toe-curling kiss department.

As quick as it started, he broke the kiss and tore free from her embrace, surprising her off balance. He grabbed her upper arms to steady her, stared at her lips as if he wanted to kiss her again, cursed, and...strode out the door. She flinched as the bedroom door slammed behind him. What the hell?

Okay, she thought as she huffed out a shaky breath and gathered her wits, *the man is crazy. One-hundred percent, certi-fricken-fiably nuts.* She dug her fingers into her temples as her headache returned full blast. If she never laid eyes on that arrogant SOB again it would be way too soon. But...damn if a little part of her didn't want to chase after him. Instead, she strengthened her resolve and forced herself into the bathroom for a couple of aspirin and a hot bath.

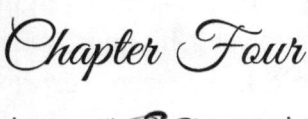

Chapter Four

"You've been awful quiet this morning."

Drew cast his sister a sidelong glance from under the hood of her car. "That a crime?"

"No. Just odd." Hannah stepped around to stand beside him. "So?"

"So what?"

She bumped him with her hip. "So what's got you in such a snit?"

With a sigh, he stood and wiped his hands on his uniform. "Snit?"

Hannah grinned.

"I have a better question—what's going on with that idiot, Swan? He finally get the message to stay the hell away from you?"

Her grin disappeared. "I told you, I'm handling it."

"Hannah, if he's giving you a hard time—"

Suddenly, Bo went nuts barking his fool head off. Drew groaned as a familiar white furball ran into the garage and headed straight for Bo. The thing rubbed between his legs, purring so loudly Drew wouldn't have been surprised if it took flight. Then it fell to its back and rolled around on the dirty, grease-stained concrete floor, writhing and stretching while Bo whined his approval.

Great. Just friggin' perfect. Thank God the furball's "mommy" wasn't here. Maybe Drew'd have time to get the thing washed and dried before she showed up. "All right, kitty, enough. You're officially as filthy as you can get." Drew swatted at the cat, but Bo growled his displeasure, shocking the shit out of him. "So it's like that, is it? Good God, mutt, she's a *cat*. You can't mate with a cat."

A feminine shriek split the air, and Drew glanced up just in time to see Lindy rush in. *Ah, shit.* She shot him a look that sent his nuts north for cover, then rushed toward the two lovebirds. Only her boot hit the same oil slick her cat had bathed in, and she went up and came crashing down—right on her ass. Drew rushed forward to help her up.

"I'm so sorry. I haven't had a chance to sprinkle oil dry down yet. You all right?"

Lindy slapped his hand away and climbed slowly to her feet. Craning her neck, she tried to check her butt. A huge black spot saturated each cheek. She brushed uselessly at the stains before pinning him with that same haughty stare that never failed to turn him on. Drew had to fight to keep his expression impassive.

"I'll pay to have them cleaned. Just send me the bill."

"Keep your money. And keep that monster of a dog away from my baby."

Drew propped his hands on his hips. "Hey, whoa. Your stupid cat ran in here, onto *my* property. If you'd keep the friggin' thing on a leash, this wouldn't have happened."

Her face screwed up in comical dismay. "You're saying this is my fault?"

"Who else? Bo didn't go looking for that furball. She came sniffing around for him."

"Ass." Lindy scooped up her cat and cuddled the grimy thing against her chest. She turned to Hannah, effectively dismissing him. "I don't suppose you have a pet groomer here in Mayberry?"

Hannah's grin returned as she cast a questioning look at Drew. "I have no idea where

Mayberry is, but Beverly Donovan does pet grooming out of her home. She lives on Liberation Lane, the street just off of Salvation, right behind the library. You can't miss it; there's a statue of Jesus on her front lawn, and she has gold and green shutters."

When Lindy cocked a brow, Hannah added, "Her husband was a huge Packers fan."

"Oh." Lindy sent Drew a quick condemning look, then turned back to his sister. "Thank you, Hannah."

She carefully stepped over the oil puddle she'd slipped on, accepted a stack of paper towels from Hannah, and strode out the door, Bianca howling her displeasure with each step.

Bo's answering whine had Drew rolling his eyes. He gave Mr. Pathetic a pat on the head and assured him, "You're better off without her, boy. Trust me. Once she got bored with you, that female would stomp your heart to mush and feed it to you for breakfast."

Hannah cleared her throat, though the sound more closely resembled a chuckle.

"What?"

"Oh, nothing." She pulled open the heavy metal door that opened into the breezeway of their home, then looked back over her shoulder. Her knowing smile really chafed his ass. "I just wonder if you plan to take your own advice." She shut the door without waiting for a reply. A full minute must have passed while he stared at the closed door in frustrated silence.

"Women," he finally muttered. "Crazy, the whole lot of 'em."

"Anyone I know?" The question was followed by a loud *"Woof!"*

Drew swung his head, surprised to see his buddy Charlie Russell standing just inside the service door, Sugar, Bo's sister, at his heel. "Christ, I didn't even hear you come in."

"Interesting considering Sugar practically took the door down on her way in." Charlie let Sugar off her leash, and she ran straight for Bo, who barked his excitement as brother and sister went at it, sniffing, nipping, roughhousing. "So again, anyone I know?" Understanding flared in his eyes accompanied by a knowing grin. "Ahh. The lovely Miss Melinda Spalding. Got you twisted up already, hey?"

Scowling, Drew got back to work on Hannah's Jeep. "Why does everyone refer to her like that? *Miss Melinda Spalding,*" he mimicked. "As if she's so damn special."

Charlie chuckled as he joined Drew under the hood. "Damn, it's even worse than I thought."

"Shut the hell up." Drew cast his grinning friend a sidelong glare. "Besides, this ain't about *her*, it's about her stupid cat and my idiot dog. Something weird's going on. I swear it's like they're in love or something."

"Maybe you should take him to see Dana. She specializes in that kinda stuff."

Drew thought about it for a second. Charlie's fiancée had lots of fancy degrees, and the vet raved about her. Seemed kind of strange to bring a dog to a shrink, though. But what other choice did he have? Bo's infatuation with a pretty face could only end in heartbreak. And it was his job to make sure that didn't happen, right?

"Guess it can't hurt. Anything to get that annoying female out of our lives."

"You talking about the cat or the woman?"

"Both. Now make yourself useful and hand me that flathead."

"I swear, Bianca, I have no idea what you were thinking. Rolling around on that disgusting concrete floor like some common...some common housecat! Your bloodlines go all the way back to the days of the

Crusaders, for God's sake. I expected better from you, young lady. Much better."

Bianca gave an owlish blink and let out a pathetic "*mrow*" before giving her paw a lick; more for show than anything else, Lindy knew. Good Lord, her fur was so matted down it was a miracle Bianca could even lift her head. Stupid...dog.

"And he drools. Is that really what you want?" Lindy tsked. "You can do so much better, girl. Trust mommy. We'll get you cleaned up, and once you've had time to think about it, you'll see that I'm right. Maybe we should start looking for a suitable companion for you. A nice Himalayan with an impeccable pedigree. Would you like that?"

"Rooow!"

Lindy made a left onto the street just before the library, then another quick left onto Liberation Lane. Beverly Donovan's house was easy enough to spot, just as Hannah said it would be. Besides the Jesus statue and green and yellow shutters, a huge 'Go, Pack, Go!' sign hung in the front picture window. Lindy pulled into the driveway and killed the engine, praying the woman was home.

With a paper towel-wrapped Bianca held firmly against her chest, she hurried up the

DONNA MARIE ROGERS

walkway, relieved to hear music coming from inside the house. "Looks like we're in luck, girl," she said and rapped on the door. It swung open, and an attractive middle-aged woman stood there, her expression curious, her dark brown eyes widening when they landed on Bianca. She wore a powder blue velour jogging suit, and her graying blonde hair piled on top of her head in a loose bun.

"Well, there's no reason to ask why you're here, is there?" Beverly said with a chuckle, her singsong voice light and airy, surprisingly soothing. Lindy smiled. There was something quite charming about the older lady.

She gave Bianca a reassuring cuddle. "Mrs. Donovan, my name is Melinda Spalding and this is Bianca. I was told that you do pet grooming out of your home...?"

"That I do, love. Come on in. And please, call me Bev."

"Thank you." Lindy stepped into the small foyer and followed Bev through the kitchen, where the rich scent of cinnamon mingled with the nutty aroma of freshly brewed coffee. Lindy breathed deep, eager for a sample of whatever it was that smelled so yummy.

"Cinnamon rolls," Bev supplied, as if reading her mind. "My oldest son will be here soon with

52

my granddaughter. He's a single dad, so I watch her full-time during the week while he's at work."

"Oh, I'm sorry, I should've called first. I could come back...?"

"Nonsense. You're already here, may as well stay. Besides, that poor thing looks as miserable as my Paco when he can't remember where he's buried his bone." With a 'follow me' wave, Bev led her through the living room to a small backroom which appeared to be her laundry room.

"You have a lovely home," Lindy said and meant it. Though the outside was a tad tacky in her opinion, the interior could have been right out of Style magazine. Brushed stainless steel appliances graced the kitchen, along with granite countertops, gleaming walnut cabinets, and polished hardwood floors. The living room was striking in brass and glass with a sleek, modern black leather sofa and matching loveseat.

"Thank you. My husband loved remodeling. I swear the man was always working on one project or another. Redid the bathroom three times, the kitchen twice. And my daughter is an interior designer, so she's constantly buying things for me."

Bev turned on the faucet in the utility sink and tested the temperature before plugging it to fill. "All right, sweetheart, time for your bath." She carefully took Bianca from Lindy's arms. Bianca looked back over her shoulder and let loose a pitiful whine as Bev set her in the sink.

"Sorry, Binks," Lindy gently chided. "You have no one to blame but yourself." She moved in closer to give Bianca a reassuring scratch behind the ears.

"My goodness," the older lady said as she squeezed pet shampoo into her hand. "How in the world did you get so dirty anyway? Looks like you were rolling around in a grease pit."

"She was, sort of." Lindy explained about Bianca's unnatural attraction to Drew Porter's mangy monster of a dog and her escape earlier from *Coffee To Chai For* to go see him.

A knowing smile lit the older woman's eyes as she lathered and scrubbed the top of Bianca's head with nimble hands. "Got yourself a crush, eh? Not that I blame you. That is one fine looking dog." She met Lindy's gaze for a brief moment. "And his master ain't too hard on the eyes either."

"Hmph. I guess. If you like the rude, rough-and-tumble type. Frankly, I prefer a man a little less acerbic. And some manners would be nice."

"Are we talking about the same Drew Porter? Because the young man I know has never been anything but kind and pleasant."

Lindy eyed the older woman with skepticism. Before she could voice a reply, a masculine voice called out, "Mom? We're here!"

"Oh, that would be Mike and Maddie." She turned and called out, "I'm in the back room!"

A moment later, a little girl with a mop of red curls and freckled cheeks skidded to a halt inside the grooming slash laundry room. Her gaze bounced from Lindy to the sink where her grandmother was elbow deep in suds. Bianca let loose with a rather loud *mrow*, and a huge smile lit up the little girl's face, revealing the cutest dimples Lindy had ever seen. Maddie scampered forward to lean against her grandmother's hip and peer into the sink.

"Careful, sweetie. She's not too happy at the moment."

"I won't pet her, Nana, I promise."

Watching the heartwarming scene before her, Lindy's heart swelled with a yearning completely foreign to her. Children weren't exactly a priority for her—heck, she wasn't even dating anyone at the moment. Not to mention she was only twenty-five years old. But there was something about Maddie...the way she gazed up at her grandmother, leaned into her side, her excitement over watching Bianca get a bath. That sweet face, those adorable curls. All of it doing funny things to Lindy's maternal mojo, making her ache for things she'd never given much thought to before—home, hearth, a family of her own.

Dammit...fricken Mayberry already!

She glanced up in time to see a uniformed police officer striding their way, a coffee mug in one hand, a gooey cinnamon roll in the other. He eyed her with smiling curiosity as he approached. *So this is Mike, huh? Not bad, not bad at all. Bet he wouldn't push me away if I kissed him.*

Too bad the only man you want to kiss is an overbearing, egotistical jackass.

"Hi."

Lindy's cheeks crooked up of their own accord. The man really was something. What a smile. "Hi."

Bev glanced over her shoulder. "Ah, good, you helped yourself. Mike, I'd like you to meet Melinda Spalding. Melinda, this is my son, Mike. Also known as Officer Donovan."

He grinned. "I'd shake your hand, but..." He gestured helplessly with the mug and the cinnamon roll.

"I understand. Those look and smell delicious."

"Oh, crud!" Bev craned her neck and gave Lindy a look of apology. "I didn't even think to offer you one. Such a dunderhead I am. Mike, would you mind? Pour her a cup of coffee, too, please."

"No problem." His eyes twinkled with amusement. "Melinda, how do you take your coffee?"

Chapter Five

"Hmm...I think I'll try the turkey club, with steak fries and a large glass of lemonade." Lindy folded the menu and handed it back to Hannah.

Hannah tucked the menu under her arm with a nod and a rueful smile. "Listen, I'm really sorry about Bianca. Was Bev able to clean her up?"

Lindy waved off her apology. "The little stinker's good as new, so no worries. And it wasn't your fault; I should've had her on a leash. Bianca's normally very well-behaved. She's certainly never run off like that before. Though I knew exactly where she'd gone off to."

Humor lit Hannah's eyes. "They're in love. I think it's cute."

Lindy barely held back an eye-roll. "They're of different species."

"I know. But come on, don't you find it just the teensiest bit romantic?"

Now Lindy did roll her eyes. "Hannah, I think your bun may be twisted too tight."

With a soft laugh, Hannah walked off to place Lindy's order. It amazed her that such a nice, thoughtful girl was related to that foul-tempered jackass.

As if you have such a sweet disposition. Pffft.

Oh, shut up.

Lindy opened her laptop and found the file she wanted. Hannah returned with her lemonade and a bottle of ketchup. "Your club and fries will be up in a few minutes."

When Hannah remained standing at her side, Lindy looked up and was met by curious mirth. "You're obviously dying to ask me something."

Hannah cast a quick glance over her shoulder before sliding into the booth across from her. "I can't remember the last time I saw my brother like that. What the heck did you do to him?"

Lindy gaped at her. "Me? Why would you assume *I* did something to *him*? Maybe that arrogant brother of yours...what's so funny?"

Hannah's grin broadened. "You've got it as bad as he does. Why don't you two just admit there's something there and see where it goes?"

Because I don't plan to stay in town long enough to find out. "Look, I understand. You're a romantic at heart and you'd like to see that playboy brother of yours settle down. But—"

"Drew isn't a playboy."

"—trust me when I say—"

"He just hasn't found the right woman yet."

"—I'm not the one for him. And he surely isn't the man for me."

Frustration creased Hannah's brow, but she held her gaze in thoughtful silence. With a reluctant nod, she stood. "Okay, then, I won't push. But I think you're wrong. You're exactly what my brother needs. And whether you want to admit it or not, I think he's exactly what you need, too." With that, Hannah headed back to the kitchen.

Clacking her nails on the table in exasperation, Lindy stared after the younger girl, the truth of her words sinking in like boulders in quicksand. Only in her own mind could Lindy admit her attraction to Drew had soared past the physical and landed with a thud in the deep end of the pool. She wanted him, had since the first moment she'd laid eyes on the arrogant man. And with just one kiss—one unforgettable, heart-stopping kiss—she'd started to yearn for him in ways she'd never before experienced. The magnitude of emotion that had swelled in her chest after that kiss scared the hell out of her.

Regardless, Lindy couldn't fathom the thought of settling here in the Midwest. L.A. was her home—always had been, always would be. The beautiful climate, amazing and diverse restaurants, numerous historical museums, shopping on Rodeo Drive. Not to mention the breathtaking backdrop of the Santa Monica Mountains. And she knew it'd be a cold day in Hell before Drew Porter packed up and moved to the City of Angels with her. So really, what would be the point of pursuing something that could never be more than a fling?

Hannah delivered her lunch with another sheepish grin, and Lindy realized with a start that Drew wasn't the only resident of Mayberry she was becoming attached to. Heck, several members of this tiny town had burrowed under her skin—from the Porters, to most of Matt and Carrie's friends, to even the gruff old man who owned this diner. Redemption was a great place filled with even better people, and she grimaced over the realization that she was being sucked in more and more each day.

Giving herself a mental shake, Lindy took a bite of her sandwich and got back to work on her laptop. She hadn't written anything in well over a month and figured some new scenery would start her creative juices flowing again. If she didn't have the first draft to her editor by June 1st, there'd be hell to pay.

Vanessa spun away, waving off Bianca's suggestion as preposterous. As if she would so much as look at that scoundrel, let alone ask for his help. The man was as arrogant as they came, not to mention boorish. And a rogue. A handsome rogue, yes, but a rogue nonetheless. Sure, he could charm the stars from the sky with just one mesmerizing look, but she had her pride. Countess Vanessa Magville would get on her knees for no man, most especially Sir Andrew Portland. She'd rather—

A low squeal brought Lindy's head around with a snap. She groaned as she met Hannah's wide-eyed gaze. Crapola, she hadn't heard her come up behind her! Okay, no need to panic, she assured herself. Really, what were the chances Hannah was a fan of romance novels let alone a fan of—

"Oh, my God, you're Katelynn Meadows!"

Shit. Seemed chances were excellent. "Could you announce it a little louder? I don't think the western half of the state heard you."

Hannah bent over the booth and eagerly scanned the computer screen, eyes bright with excitement, her bottom lip caught between her teeth. Lindy couldn't hold back a smile. Nothing made an author happier than an excited fan, and it seemed she had at least one here in Mayberry.

"You're writing Vanessa's story! Oh, my God, I was praying Vanessa would get her own..." A howl of laughter suddenly erupted from Hannah, drawing several sets of probing eyes in their direction. Lindy glanced around, avoiding direct eye contact as she prayed for the linoleum to open up and swallow her whole. She slammed her laptop shut and glared at Hannah.

Holding a hand over her mouth as if to keep from laughing, Hannah's eye danced with delight. "Sir Andrew Portland? You named a character after him."

"Don't be absurd," Lindy hotly denied. "It's purely coincidental."

"Uh-huh. Sure." Hannah's knowing grin was really starting to grate. "Does anyone else know? I imagine Matt and Carrie—"

"No one knows, and I'd like to keep it that way, please." Lindy hoped her expression conveyed just how serious she was about this. No one could find out about Katelynn Meadows until the time was right. She needed to let her family in on her secret before the public found out or she'd never hear the end of it. Especially since she planned to start writing full-time once the plant was up and running. News which would not go over well with her parents.

Especially her father, who was still recovering from a major heart attack.

"Seriously?" Hannah's face screwed up with genuine confusion. "But you should be proud. You're a NY Times bestselling author. Your Magville series was featured in People magazine. Why wouldn't you want anyone to know that?"

"I know it's hard to understand, but I have my reasons. Anyway, it won't be for much longer. Think you can keep my secret a few more months?"

"Of course. If that's what you want." A sudden grin chased away Hannah's contemplative frown. "I can't wait to see the look on Drew's face when he finds out. He's always teasing me about reading 'that crap'."

Great. Yet another reason to despise the man. Not that she needed one...the jackass.

Hannah turned to leave, but then spun back around. "I meant to tell you. Charlie's fiancée, Dana McClain, works at the vet office and deals with animal behavioral problems. I bet she could help with Bianca's odd attraction to my brother's dog."

"I swear, I must be nuts," Drew muttered as he dragged a leashed Bo into the veterinarian's office. Rick Wilde stood behind the counter showing Mrs. Baiker how to apply oral hygiene rinse to her miniature collie's teeth with a gauze pad. Bo jerked on his leash, desperate to get the hell out of there, but Drew held tight. Good things didn't usually happen at the vet's office, and Bo had a long memory.

Mrs. Baiker paid for her purchase and smiled at Drew on her way past. Bo gave the miniature collie a nose in the ass as was his usual custom.

"Drew, good to see you." Rick shook his hand before giving Bo a pat on the head. "Hey, buddy, looking good. So what brings you guys in?"

Clearing his throat, Drew admitted, "We're here to see Dana. Bo has...issues."

Rick did his best to hide his grin. "You don't say. Well, Dana just started a session with another patient, so you'll have a bit of a wait, I'm afraid."

Before Drew could reply, the door to Dana's office opened and she stuck her head out. "Drew, Bo, if you're ready, you can come on in."

Without warning, Bo went nuts, nearly ripping Drew's arm from its socket in his quest to reach Dana. "Okay, okay, I'm coming. Christ, two minutes ago I had to drag your ass in here."

"Now that he's seen Dana, he probably thinks Sugar's in there. Have a good session." Rick gave Drew a thump on the shoulder before waving his next patient into his office.

Drew let Bo lead the way, thankful the big oaf was too preoccupied to goose Mrs. Allen as he barreled toward Dana's office. As soon as Dana closed the door behind them, Drew realized who the other occupants were. Sitting in the chair closest to the wall was Lindy, that troublesome white fluff ball perched on her lap. And her less than enthused expression said she was just as surprised to see him.

Bo and Bianca both went wild—barking, howling, struggling to break free, frantic to reach each other. Drew held tight, marveling over how strong Bo'd become over the past several months. He shot a quick glance at Hot Stuff, who was having a similar problem holding onto her cat.

"The door is shut, so they can't escape and run off together. Drew, why don't you have a seat next to Lindy, and we'll let these two enjoy each other's company while we talk."

"But that's the problem. I don't want my baby anywhere near this monster. He's a bad influence." Lindy shot Drew a look of contempt.

"Hey, if anyone's a bad influence it's that spoiled rotten furball you call a cat. Showing up at the garage, rolling around in the dirt like some—"

"Watch it, *Lou*, or you'll have to have my boot surgically removed from your—"

"Okay," Dana quickly interrupted. "This is where we all take a deep, calming breath. After hearing the basics from Melinda, I decided to combine your sessions and face the problem head on."

Reluctant to even be there, let alone have to share space with Matt's infuriating sister, Drew wanted nothing more than to get it all over and done with so he—and Bo—could move the hell on. Lindy and her puffball would be on their way back to California in a few short months, and it was best for everyone if they simply let Dana do her thing and cure Bo of his ridiculous infatuation.

With a hesitant nod, Lindy set Bianca on the floor. Bo sniffed her from nose to tail, and then rolled onto his back with an enthusiastic bark. Loud purring joined Bo's happy grunt as the two rolled, rubbed, and loved on each other.

"Repulsive," Lindy murmured, watching them through narrowed eyes.

For some odd reason Drew was feeling ornery. "The only thing repulsive is your bad attitude."

Lindy slapped a hand against the arm of her chair, and spun to face him, eyes wide with indignation. "My bad attitude? *My* bad attitude? You...you..."

Satisfied to have gotten a rise out of her, Drew taunted, "You-you what? Come on, Hot Stuff, spit it out."

"You idiot! I swear God was punishing me the day he tossed you into my life. You're arrogant and bad-mannered and...you smell like motor oil!"

"I'm an auto mechanic, princess. What do you expect me to smell like, roses?"

Lindy slammed back into her chair with a huff, and crossed her arms.

Drew cocked a teasing brow at Dana. "Aren't you supposed to say, 'And how does that make you feel?'"

Dana grinned. "No, it's perfectly clear how both of you feel. But perhaps we could get back to Bo and Bianca...?"

For some reason, the fact that Lindy was in such a foul mood brought out his mischievous side. Lacing his fingers behind his head, elbows out, he drawled, "I agree. And now that I've thought about it, who are we to stand in the way of true love?"

"Excuse me?" Lindy shot forward so fast one of her hair combs flew from her head and clattered across the floor.

Dana leaned over to pick it up and set it on her desk.

"Have you lost your feeble mind? No way are you going to encourage a relationship between these two!"

The 'two' in question took a break from bathing each other to gaze up at Lindy, ears cocked with curiosity. Drew had to admit, he envied their ease with each other. Be nice if Hot Stuff stole a page from her cat's book and tried a little honey instead of the vinegar that normally spewed from her lips.

Except when she'd kissed him. Her lips had been pretty damn sweet then. *Shit.*

"Jesus, woman, chill out before you scare off the patients in the waiting room."

"I swear, in about two seconds I'm going to beat you to a pulp with the heel of my boot, you—"

"O-kay," Dana interrupted for a second time, an unmistakable chuckle in her voice. "Again, we need to calm down and take a deep breath." She demonstrated before standing up and coming around her desk to stand before them. Her gaze dropped to the lovebirds. Bo was sprawled out on his side with Bianca now lying across his neck, one paw resting on his big head as if holding him in place while she thoroughly cleaned his ear. Drew shuddered at the sight, but Bo was in heaven, with his tongue lolling out of his mouth and his hind leg going like a windmill.

Lindy shifted uncomfortably in her chair. "I'm sorry, Dana, I know you mean well, but I'm not so sure this was a good idea." Lindy shot Drew a sidelong glance before adding, "Sometimes, two...animals, no matter how attracted they are to each other, shouldn't be together."

"And why is that?" Drew demanded. Her constant negative attitude was really starting to grate on his nerves.

"You don't want them spending time together anymore than I do," Lindy reminded him, her tone pure ice. "So what's with the one-eighty?"

Before he could respond, Dana jumped in. "Listen, I have an idea that I think might work, though it may sound a little unconventional at first. Will you hear me out?" When they both nodded, she continued. "The forbidden can be an incredible aphrodisiac. Eventually, just like us humans, the more time they spend together, the more the charm will wear off. I'd suggest you set up a couple of play dates. Let them spend plenty of time together, eventually, they'll get tired of each other."

Suspicious by nature, Drew wasn't sure if he completely bought Dana's 'solution'. But not so much as a facial twitch gave away any ulterior motives. He glanced at Lindy who sat in surprising silence considering Dana's suggestion would mean *they'd* have to spend more time together as well. Deciding to test her mood, he said, "Well, I'm free tonight. You?"

She hesitated, sharing a look with Dana, no doubt wracking her brain for any excuse to get out of it. "Actually, Matt and Caleb are coming over for pizza tonight. My way of thanking them for all the work they did on the house."

"That right?"

"I didn't think you'd be interested," she added, her tone defensive.

"Come on, Hot Stuff, at least be honest. You didn't ask because you didn't want me there."

"Hey," she reminded him, "you're the one who ran out of my house like your hair was on fire. Why would I assume you'd want to come back after that?"

"You don't have to explain, I get it." He'd done plenty of work on that house, and she damn well knew it.

"Fine." She blew a frustrated sigh through her nose. "Would you and Bo like to join us for pizza tonight? Around seven?"

Drew looked down at Bo who let out two loud barks. "Bo says if you're ordering Nino's, he'll take an order of chicken strips. Extra ranch dressing."

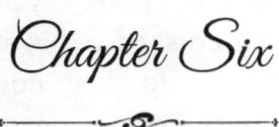

Chapter Six

"So what would you guys like on your pizza?"

Curled up on the sofa in the living room, Lindy had her cell phone in one hand and the menu for Nino's in the other. Matt and Caleb had arrived early so they could finish up some odd and end jobs before the house was officially complete. Carrie couldn't make it because she was having dinner with her parents, and Caleb's fiancée, Lauren, was home with two sick kids.

"I'm easy," Caleb said as he cracked open a beer. "The only thing I don't like is anchovies."

Matt snatched the menu from her hand and perused it before announcing, "I think I'll have that beef sandwich I had a taste for the other day. Hot peppers and extra au jus on the side. And make sure you get an appetizer basket."

"I like sausage and mushrooms," Lindy said, grabbing the menu back. "Don't suppose either of you know what Drew likes on his pizza...?"

Unbidden, the feel of Drew's lips on hers, the memory of being crushed in his strong embrace nearly rocked her to her core. Then she remembered how he'd shoved away from her and raced out the damn door—

"Matter of fact, he likes sausage and mushroom, too," Matt told her before taking a swig of his beer. "And Bo likes chicken strips."

"You don't actually expect me to order food for his dog, do you?" The very idea was absurd.

"Why not? Bo'll be thrilled, and it'll score you a few points with Drew." Matt gave her an exaggerated wink and Caleb wiggled his eyebrows suggestively.

Lindy slapped them both with the menu. "I don't want to score any points with Drew or his monster of a dog. I just want to eat this meal as quickly as possible, then fake a stomach ache and head up to bed."

Matt and Caleb both chuckled, and even Lindy couldn't hide her smile.

"Well, he and I can't seem to get along for more than five seconds, so it just seems like the smart thing to do—avoid him as much as possible."

"Which is why you invited him over for pizza tonight," Matt pointed out like the smartass he was.

"I told you, it was Dana's idea. She thinks if we let Bo and Binks spend time together, eventually they'll get sick of each other. Though I have to admit, I think she may be full of shit."

Matt let out a bark of laughter and promptly choked on his beer. Caleb gave him a thump on the back.

"Sorry." Lindy grinned. "All right, I'm ordering. It'll take at least forty minutes to arrive, and Drew is due here in about thirty." Lindy called to place the order, meeting Matt's knowing smirk with a roll of her eyes as she added on an order of chicken strips with extra ranch dressing.

After chatting for a little while about all the work they'd done on the house, the guys headed into the kitchen for fresh beers—and of course that's when she heard the hum of Drew's pickup as it pulled into the driveway. Crap, he was early. She'd wanted to run upstairs and change into sweats and a T-shirt before they ate so she didn't get anything on her silk blouse. And with

Bo around, it was pretty much a given something gross would end up splattered all over her.

Bianca tore down the stairs howling her little heart out and skidded to a halt beside the door. Lindy shook her head as she followed behind, still completely baffled by the connection between her elegant purebred cat and that mammoth train wreck of a dog. Bo barked a greeting as he rushed across the snow-covered lawn, then leapt onto the porch and raced inside.

"Hussy," Lindy teased as Bianca swished her backside in Bo's face. The two danced over to the roaring fireplace, collapsed onto the rug, and got busy bathing each other. A smile touched Lindy's lips. Though she'd never admit it out loud, it tickled her to see Bianca so happy. And Bo'd been slowly worming his way under her skin—just like his way too handsome for his own good master.

Both revelations would have to stay firmly planted in her own head, however, since nothing could come of either scenario. She and Bianca would be heading back to L.A. just as soon as her work here was done. The longer she stayed, the harder it would be to leave.

Maybe she needed to follow Dana's advice, only in reverse, and stay the hell away from Drew before she lost what little sanity—and self-respect—she had left. He'd already demonstrated what little regard he had for her when he'd kissed her and then tossed her back, as if she were a fish that wasn't quite big enough to keep.

Fish analogies? Sheesh, maybe she needed to head back to L.A. tonight.

Drew stomped the snow from his boots before stepping inside and handing her a bottle of champagne. He looked uncomfortable, which surprised her. Now what could make the overbearingly confident Drew Porter look as nervous as a Kindergartner on the first day of school? And champagne? She'd have sooner expected him to hand her a six-pack of beer.

He cleared his throat. "Thought you might want to have a glass to celebrate."

"That was very thoughtful, thank you. Matt and Caleb are in the kitchen. Would you mind putting the champagne in the fridge while I run upstairs and change?" There, that sounded civil, right? Friendly even.

Drew's brow creased just the tiniest bit before a smile transformed that usually frowning mouth. "Will do."

Whistling softly, he strode off toward the kitchen, and Lindy hurried up to her bedroom to change. For some unfathomable reason, the urge to slip into a slinky LBD struck, but she resisted. No sense tempting fate. Instead, she threw on a pair of baby blue sweats and a matching long-sleeve T-shirt. After combing her hair up into a ponytail, she padded back downstairs.

The doorbell rang and she hurried over to answer it, grateful the food was on time. Bo let out a couple of half-hearted barks as she swung open the door, then went right back to being pampered by her hussy of a cat. The thought brought an unexpected smile to her face.

The delivery guy returned the smile, no doubt assuming it had been for him, and hefted the pizza box and other food. "Evenin'. Your total comes to $47.56."

"Come on in, I have to grab my purse from the kitchen."

"Wow. Nice place."

He glanced around with interest, and Lindy felt a sense of pride that caught her off guard. She'd decided to purchase a home in Redemption because with her brother living here, she—and their parents—would be making somewhat regular visits. And there wasn't a five-star hotel within a hundred mile radius. Besides, as soon as she opened the email containing a picture of Kendall Manor, she'd been sold. This was her house and she loved it.

Maybe too much.

"Thank you."

She retrieved her purse from the kitchen and saw the guys out on the back porch fixing a broken step. Lindy slid open the patio door to announce the food had arrived, then rushed back to the foyer to pay for it. She stopped short, surprised to discover the delivery driver staring intently at the oil painting she'd picked up in Milan last year.

"Sorry about the wait," she said as she approached, feeling the slightest niggle of unease. She handed him sixty dollars. "Keep the change."

"Cool, thanks a lot." He pocketed the money and handed Lindy the stack of hot cardboard boxes. Goosebumps broke out on her skin as she watched him hop in his car and take off, though she had no idea why he made her feel so uncomfortable.

Shaking off the feeling, she headed for the kitchen when it struck her that something wasn't quite right. She glanced at the hall table where she'd set her diamond tennis bracelet. It was gone.

Drew figured it was about time he go check on Bo, make sure he hadn't chewed up any of the new furniture. He found Lindy staring at the small table in the hall, her brow crinkled in confusion.

"What's up?" he asked, taking the boxes from her. "Mmm, man, there's nothing like the smell of Nino's." When she didn't respond, he touched her arm. "You all right?"

"Huh? Oh, yeah. Sorry. It's just..." She glanced up at him, then back at the table. "My bracelet is missing. The clasp broke, and I set it in this dish because I'd planned on calling a jeweler in the morning. Now it's gone."

"Sure you didn't take it upstairs? Or maybe put it in your purse?"

"I'm positive. I put it right here." She looked up at him again, her expression grim. "I think the delivery guy stole it."

He cocked a brow. "That's a bit of a leap, don't you think?"

"No, it's not. You didn't see the way he was looking around, as if trying to figure out what everything is worth."

"Hot Stuff, this is a really nice house, but it's not like you have anything of real value here, right?"

"Wrong. I have thousands of dollars worth of jewelry upstairs in my room. And that painting," she pointed to the framed canvas hanging over the fireplace, "is worth almost twenty grand. I think he knew that."

Twenty Gs for a painting? Maybe he should've paid more attention in sixth grade art class. "We're talking about a kid who delivers pizza for a living. How could he possibly know what some fancy painting is worth?"

"I don't know, and he wasn't some kid. He was a grown man, at least in his mid-twenties. And shifty looking. I left to get my purse from the kitchen, and when I came back he was staring at that painting. He really left me with a bad feeling."

Drew glanced around at the sparse furnishings. "To be fair, there's not much else to look at. A few knickknacks, a couple of paintings that would be pretty hard to get rid of unless someone had major connections."

"The whole town knows who Matt and I are," she countered. "It wouldn't take a rocket scientist to figure out I might have some valuable items in this house."

She definitely had a point, though he hated to admit the possibility that Nino had a thief working for him. "I'll tell you what. If your bracelet doesn't show up by tomorrow, I'll talk to Nino myself, all right?"

With a reluctant nod, Lindy strode past him, leading the way into the kitchen. Matt and

Caleb had just finished up with the back porch step, and they all entered the kitchen at the same time. Lindy gathered plates and forks while Drew opened the pizza box and the rest of the food containers.

"Lindy ordered the chicken strips for Bo," Matt pointed out, smiling as she plunked the plates and forks on the table.

She eyeballed Matt before grudgingly meeting Drew's gaze with a nonchalant shrug. "Everyone needs to eat, even that monster in there. Better chicken strips than my furniture."

"Come on, Hot Stuff, admit it. Bo's growing on you."

"Yeah, like mold."

Ignoring her wisecrack, Drew whistled for Bo. And just to prove what a gentleman he could be, Drew fed him the chicken strips one at a time. Bo took each one from Drew's hand with gentle care, even dropping one on the floor for his lady love. The finicky feline sniffed it a couple times before hunkering down to eat with dainty nibbles.

Lindy watched with raised brows before admitting, "Okay, so his manners are better than I would've imagined."

Drew gave Bo a pat on the head, which started his tail thumping. "Don't worry, boy.

It's just a matter of time before she's completely under your spell."

"Yeah, I wouldn't count on that."

Drew shared a knowing look with Matt and Caleb.

Halfway through dinner Caleb got a call on his cell. Lauren had come down with whatever the kids had and needed him to come home ASAP. He thanked Lindy for supper, said his goodbyes, and raced out the door. Drew envied Caleb his relationship with Lauren and her kids. In just a few short months, they'd become a real family. Even with their rocky start, Max looked up to Caleb, who couldn't love the kid more if he were his own. And Caleb adored Emma, but then everyone in town loved that little cutie. The only thing missing was the wedding. Which Drew had a feeling might be coming soon.

As he gazed across the table at Lindy, his chest swelled with the same indescribable emotion he'd first experienced last summer when she'd fishtailed into his life. He'd wanted her from the moment she'd stepped out of that slick, red Ferrari. He'd thought about her almost constantly, even after she headed back to L.A. It wasn't until he'd finally convinced himself they could never have a future that he was able to extricate the blonde stunner from his thoughts. They came from two different worlds; hell, from two different galaxies.

Though judging by the way she'd kissed him, he knew she wanted him, too. But the contrary woman was as stubborn as they came. And after the way he'd hotfooted it out of here Sunday night, she'd no doubt serve him his nuts on a platter if he dared to try and pick up where they'd left off. He'd panicked, plain and simple. But of course she'd taken his leaving as a rejection. He was an idiot for running out on her the way he had, but maybe he'd get a chance to make it up to her tonight.

His contrary thoughts were giving him a headache.

"Hey, guys, I think I'm going to head home myself. Carrie'll be back soon, and dinner with her family always puts her in a mood."

"Good or bad?" Lindy asked.

Matt wriggled his eyebrows. "Depends. But there's chocolate-covered macadamia nut ice cream in the freezer, a bottle of her favorite wine in the fridge, and when all else fails, it's foot massage time."

Lindy grinned as she swiped a drop of pizza sauce from her lip with her tongue.

Drew's groin tightened at the action.

"You rock as a boyfriend, big brother. I'm impressed."

Matt tossed his keys in the air and caught them. "You know me, I pay attention." With a wink and a "See you guys later," Matt lit out of there.

They sat in silence for a few minutes, finishing their pizza, sipping on beer, looking everywhere but at each other. How ridiculous that they couldn't even look at each other. What were they, twelve?

Drew glanced at the clock. "It's only ten after eight. What do you say we crack open that champagne and watch a little tube?"

"The only TV in the house is in my bedroom."

"Even better."

Chapter Seven

"*E*xcuse me?" Lindy raised a brow at his audacity and tossed her crust onto the plate.

"We can get comfy on the bed, sip some champagne. Matt's not the only one who can give a killer foot rub, you know." He grinned, those sexy dimples doing funny things to her libido. And damn, if a foot rub didn't sound like heaven right about now.

Deciding to loosen up and enjoy herself, Lindy rose and pointed to the fridge. "You grab the champagne. I'll get the glasses."

"Hell yeah. That's what I'm talking about."

They each grabbed their items and raced for the stairs, chuckling like a couple of kids. Dozing on the rug in front of the fireplace, Bo and Bianca gave a brief lift of their heads before returning to their slumberous ecstasy.

Bottle in hand, Drew hopped onto her bed, making himself at home by kicking off his shoes and falling back against her mountain of pillows with a masculine grunt of satisfaction. And what really shocked Lindy was just how...*right* Drew looked lying on her bed.

"Damn, this is comfortable. Makes my own bed seem like a stone slab. Think it's time I invested in a new mattress."

"It's a Tempur-Pedic. They're a little on the pricier side, but well worth it."

Drew gazed at her, a disturbing intensity smoldering in his eyes. "Why don't you grab the remote and hop on up here?" He patted the space beside him. "Plenty of room on your fancy *Tempur-Pedic*."

Deciding to let his teasing remark slide, Lindy set the glasses on the end table beside him, then popped a movie in the DVD player. "Hope you're okay with horror."

"Really? And here I thought I'd have to watch a chick flick."

She gingerly climbed onto the opposite side of the bed and sat Indian style with her back ramrod straight. "Sorry to disappoint, but I have a weakness for slasher movies."

"No complaints, Hot Stuff. That was my point."

She heard the pop of the cork from the champagne and watched as Drew poured them each a glass.

The bubbly, though not Cristal or Dom Perignon quality, went down smooth, and soon she found her anxiety melting away along with her inhibitions. By the time the previews ended and the movie started, Lindy felt comfortable enough to lean back against the pillows and relax. She flexed her feet, sort of testing the waters. Yeah, this was nice. She could do this. He was just a guy...no one special.

Pffft. You want him and you know it.

Drew shifted, and suddenly they were thigh to thigh, the heat of his body warming her as awareness tingled through her veins. "More champagne?" he asked as he topped off his own glass.

"Maybe just a little."

"Can't save champagne, darlin', so drink up."

He filled her glass to within a hair of the rim. And he'd called her darlin'. Though if she were being honest, she didn't really mind being called Hot Stuff. Made her feel kind of sexy, which she hadn't felt in...well, a long time.

She sucked the bubbly down in half the time it took to sip the first glass, and then twirled it beneath his nose for more. She grinned, relaxed and cozy. He grinned back and poured her another.

They watched the movie in silence. Lindy found herself leaning Drew's way as the heroine on screen ran for her life toward the sanctuary of her car in the nearly empty mall parking lot. She managed to cram the key in the lock a split second before the killer caught her by the back of the hair. Her bloodcurdling scream rent the air as fate became a reality. The killer slapped a hand over her mouth as his bowie knife plunged into her back.

"I still can't believe you like these kinds of movies." Drew stretched his legs before casting her a sidelong glance.

"Why's that?"

He shrugged. "Chicks getting cut to shreds by some psycho nut? Didn't think in a million years you'd care for it."

"I love blood and guts movies. Always have. Used to watch them with my Grandma Kate."

He stared at her for a second. "Hot Stuff, just when I think I have you figured out, you surprise the hell out of me."

It was Lindy's turn to shrug, though a small smile played about her lips. She loved the fact he was finally seeing her in a new light; not just as the spoiled rich girl. Though, admittedly, she hadn't shown him much else to judge her by. "Can I get some more champagne, please?"

He seemed to hesitate for a moment, then shrugged. "Sure."

After she'd drained her glass for the fourth time, Drew took it from her and declared, "I'm pretty sure you've had enough now."

"Hey, you're the one who said to drink up, Bucko."

One brow rose. "Bucko? Really?"

"Bucko...Bucko...yeah, I like it. Bu-cko. Buuu-cko. BuckoBuckoBucko." She giggled. "I love that word. It's my new favorite word. Seriously."

Drew shook his head, but a reluctant smile crooked his mouth. That perfectly perfect mouth. Man, did he have nice lips.

"Okay, I think it's time for me to leave and for you to get some sleep."

"Hel-lo." She gestured toward the champagne bottle. "We're not finished yet. You're the one who said we can't save it." After a brief attempt to snatch her glass back, Lindy broke out into a serious case of the giggles.

Drew laughed and set her glass on the nightstand. "Not much of a drinker, are you,

Hot Stuff? Sure are entertaining, though, I'll give you that."

Entertaining? She'd give the big lug entertaining... *Lug. LugLugLug.* Lindy grinned. The champagne had definitely gone to her head—as well as her libido. The naughty thoughts racing through her mind kick-started a slow burn in her core. She wanted him. Now. And she was almost positive he wanted her, too. Just one time. *Work him out of your system so you can focus on the job you came to do and get back home to L.A.*

She hiked a leg over his lap, straddling him. Drew settled his hands at her waist, looking quite surprised by her boldness. Heck, she was plenty surprised herself. She gave an experimental wiggle, drawing a groan from him.

"Christ, darlin', I'm not made of stone."

She wiggled again, casting him a coquettish look through her lashes. "You do a pretty good imitation."

"You're killing me, Hot Stuff."

Throwing caution to the wind, she leaned down and kissed him—just laid one on him. A low growl rumbled in his chest, and his grip tightened as he pulled her flush against his chest. He deepened the kiss, tilting his head and slanting his mouth beneath hers. Lindy's head swam; her pulse thrummed hard with need. It had been so long since she'd been with a man. Since she'd even kissed one, until Sunday, though she'd keep that bit of news to herself. Drew's ego was practically spilling from his ears as it was.

Strong hands caressed and stroked the tender muscles of her back as deft fingers wove a tingling path up her spine, sending currents of sexual energy to every nerve in her body. Nestled against his hard chest, Lindy's nipples tightened in anticipation, every inch of her aching for the incredibly sexy man she had pinned to her bed.

Without warning, Drew broke the kiss and gently slid her off of him. He sat up with a muttered curse and pulled his cell phone from his front pocket. It must have been on vibrate because she hadn't heard it ring. He listened to a message, stared at the ceiling for a moment, then stuck it back in his pocket.

"What is it? What's wrong?"

He sat up with a groan and swiped a hand through his hair. "Nothing, I...Listen, Hot Stuff, thanks for the pizza, but it's late and I have an early day tomorrow."

Before she could form a thought, Drew rolled off the bed and shot to his feet. He looked uncomfortable, and Lindy felt like crawling in a hole. He didn't want her. She'd practically thrown herself at him, and he wasn't even interested enough to take advantage of what she offered. Tears burned her eyes.

"I'll call you." With that, he left.

She heard him call for Bo once he reached the foyer. When he shut the door, it may as well have been a cannon going off, so strong was its impact.

Being rejected by the arrogant man once was one thing. But after Sunday's aborted kiss, my God, she must be the biggest fool on the planet. He'd probably been waiting since last summer for a chance to knock her off her pedestal. And fine—touché. But Lindy had been foolish enough to let him get to her. Much as she hated to admit it, her heart ached. She'd started to fall for him, and now he knew it. The humiliation of it nearly choked her.

"I'll call you."

Flipping onto her back, she pressed the heels of her hands to her eyes, desperate to stem the flow of her tears. The faint crunch of gravel reached her as he pulled out of her driveway. A sob nearly escaped, but she choked it back, along with her vulnerability. She'd die before she'd let that man make her feel like dirt. No one could hear the ache in her chest; feel the burn of her shame. And no one needed to know just how deeply she'd fallen for the jerk.

A feminine howl of complaint penetrated Lindy's depressing thoughts, and she glanced down to see Bianca gazing soulfully up at her. Binks leapt onto the bed, purring her little heart out as she butted her head against Lindy's hand. Lindy swiped away her tears, then gave Bianca the petting of a lifetime, needing the comfort only her furry best friend could provide.

"Three more months, Bianca. Then it's back home to L.A. For good."

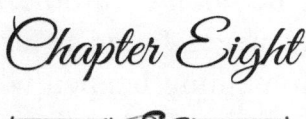

Chapter Eight

"*So* where are you off to?" Matt asked as he set Lindy's nonfat espresso macchiato to-go on the counter. Lindy pitched a five dollar bill down and snatched up her drink.

"I have to make an appearance at the plant, meet the new manager, and give dad a progress report."

Knowing better than to argue with her, Matt accepted the money and rang up her coffee. "Someone's in a mood this morning. What's up?"

"Nothing." She hooked her purse over her shoulder, careful to avoid eye contact with her perceptive older brother. Not that anyone could've missed her pissy attitude. Lord, she couldn't wait to get back to real life—which thankfully was on the other side of the country. Mayberry's small town charm and appeal had definitely started to wear off.

He eyeballed her in that annoying, 'you never could lie to me' brotherly way. The look that had never failed to draw the truth from her. "Something happen with Drew last night? You two seemed to be getting along when I left. Which, by the way, is *why* I left."

"Mind your own business."

"PMS?"

"Do you *want* to get slapped?"

Matt chuckled. "Okay, okay, I'll quit. I'm just worried about you, Lin."

She softened. "I'm fine, really. I woke up with a killer headache, and the ibuprofen hasn't kicked in yet."

"Do you want me to drive you to the plant? Jenny'll be here in half an hour and Carrie can handle this place by herself blindfolded."

"I appreciate the offer, but no. Again, I'm fine."

"Do you remember how to get there?" he pressed.

"I do. But if I forget, the new Caddy has built-in navigation."

"Good. Just remember to watch for that first left after the bridge. It's a little difficult to spot the first time. And give me a call after you meet with the plant manager. I'm curious to know what you think of him."

Matt's smile was oddly self-satisfied.

"I will," she promised. "See you later."

The plant was roughly a twenty minute ride north of Redemption, and Lindy used that time to focus on business and exorcise a certain jackass from her mind. She'd cried a few tears, tossed and turned most of the night, and now she was done. Period.

The lot sat nearly empty since they only had a skeleton crew working at the moment. Once the plant reopened, which they estimated to be May 1st, it would take over three hundred employees to run it twenty four hours a day, seven days a week. Matt had hired most of the upper management team, and as soon as Lindy made sure everything was running on course, she'd hire a full personnel team to help her fill the rest of the positions. Already, she had close to five hundred applicants, many who'd sent their resumes via email.

Lindy parked in the small lot next to the offices and glanced around with reluctant admiration as she carefully made her way across the snow-packed blacktop. Clear blue skies blanketed snow-covered pine trees for as far as the eye could see, giving the area an almost storybook enchantment. And that fresh air...she took a deep breath, let it out slowly, and frowned. Damn, she was going to miss fresh air when she headed back to the city of smog.

She unlocked the security door and stepped inside the office foyer, anxious to meet the plant manager Matt was so proud of himself for hiring. She tossed back the last swallow of her espresso macchiato, dropped the cup in the lobby trash can, and stopped to take another deep breath—this one to calm her frazzled nerves. She wondered if the plant manager was even in yet. Funny, Matt forgot to mention the guy's name, and she'd been too preoccupied to ask.

"Lindy?"

The familiar, high-pitched feminine voice came from her right. Lindy spun around and racked her brain as a gorgeous brunette strode her way, hand outstretched, smiling from ear to ear. Suddenly, it dawned on her. "Bernie?"

"I wasn't expecting you until next week!" Bernadette Mitchell, Lindy's new executive assistant, clasped her hand and nearly pumped her arm off. "It's so great to finally meet you in person."

Lindy smiled with genuine pleasure, liking the spunky woman immediately. Bernie didn't look anything like she'd imagined. Somehow she'd pictured a blonde with a beehive hairdo and big glasses.

"It's nice to meet you, too. And I'm sorry I didn't tell you I was arriving early. It was sort of a last minute decision."

Her worries were quickly waved away. "Please, no problem at all. So, what are your plans for today? Want me to start setting up interviews?"

"I'd be grateful if you did, thank you. But first I need to hire you a couple of assistants, so set those up first."

Bernie grinned. "Much appreciated."

"I'm about to go meet with the plant manager, then I have some running around to do. Any chance we can meet for dinner tonight? My treat."

"I'd love that, though you don't have to buy. Nino's has wonderful pizza and pasta. And their cannoli is the best you'll ever taste."

Lindy almost laughed aloud. These Mayberrians sure did love Italian food. You'd think Nino's was the only restaurant in town.

"Sounds good. Seven o'clock work for you? We can meet there. And I'm buying; no arguments."

Bernie's smile was appreciative. "Thanks. And FYI, Andy hasn't come out of his office since I arrived almost two hours ago."

"Andy?"

"Your plant manager."

"Oh." Lindy grimaced sheepishly. "Guess I should've known that."

Bernie did a one-shoulder shrug. "You have a lot on your mind. I'm going to start setting up those interviews for you. If I don't catch you before you leave, see you tonight."

"Looking forward to it."

The vivacious brunette turned and strode purposefully back into her office. Lindy made a quick stop in the restroom on the way, strangely anxious to meet...Andy. Geez, she still couldn't believe she'd forgotten to ask the guy's name.

The door to his office stood slightly ajar. Lindy grasped the knob just as a string of loud curses rent the air. Something struck the door with such force it slammed shut, startling her. The distinct crunch of shattering glass was quickly followed by the pungent smell of...booze?

Lindy leaned off to the side before throwing the door open. Getting beaned in the head with something wasn't exactly high on her priority list. She took a cautious peek inside, her gaze zeroing in on the middle-aged man leaning over the desk, palms braced, chest heaving. He looked up suddenly, brow raised as if startled to see her.

"What the *hell* is going on in here?" she demanded, nose wrinkled in disgust. She stepped gingerly around the broken glass, not wanting to slip in her high heels. This was Matt's brilliant plant manager? A stinking drunk?

"Who are you? Get the hell out of my office!"

Infuriated, Lindy didn't even ask for an explanation. "No, *you* get out. You're fired, effective immediately."

When he simply stood there, gaping at her in bleary-eyed silence, Lindy added, "Please don't make me call the police to escort you out of here, because if I have to, I will. Just grab your personal items and leave."

Realization dawned on who had witnessed his drunken meltdown; remorse flared in his red-rimmed blue eyes. "I'm sorry...I know how this looks, but..."

His face crumbled as he tried to explain, his demeanor having done a complete one-eighty. But Lindy didn't need to hear his excuses. What did it matter anyway? No way could she keep him in their employ after what she'd witnessed. She couldn't think of a bigger no-no, as far as Spalding Industries was concerned, than drinking on the job. Luckily for Andy it hadn't been her father who'd walked in on his little tantrum; he'd have called the police immediately and asked questions later.

"I can call you a cab if you need one, but that's the limit of my patience." Lindy glanced down at the broken glass and shook her head with regret. She met Andy's gaze, reluctant to have to explain things to Matt. He'd really been proud of this hire.

Andy straightened and dug into his front pocket. "I have my car."

"I don't think you're in any condition to drive."

Belligerence bubbled back to the surface and a scowl darkened his otherwise handsome face. Andy must have been at least in his fifties considering he'd ran the plant all those years ago, though he didn't look a day over forty. "'Course I can drive! I only had a few—" he hiccupped "—mouthfuls."

Lindy was doubtful of his ability to drive, and she certainly wasn't going to let him risk hurting himself or someone else. "Either I call you a cab or I'll call the police to escort you home. Your choice."

He eyed her with utter contempt. Not that Lindy didn't understand his anger, but once he sobered up he'd realize he had no one to blame but himself and his disgraceful behavior.

"I'll call my son."

She nodded and eyed the broken glass one last time. "I'll make sure your last paycheck is sent directly to your home." With that, Lindy shut the door behind her and stormed from the building.

"You what?" Matt looked up in surprise.

"I fired him."

"You fired him?"

"Yes, I fired him. I found the man drinking on the job."

"He was drinking?"

Lindy rolled her eyes. "Good Lord, Matt, are you going to repeat everything I say?"

Matt swiped his fingers through his hair and gave a cautious look around before leading

Lindy to the table in the corner near some book shelves. "I'm sorry, it's just...are you sure you didn't misinterpret things? You do have a habit of jumping to conclusions."

Lindy slapped her purse on the table and dropped onto a chair. "I do not. And no, I didn't jump to anything. I was about to enter the office when he threw a bottle against the door. The odor was unmistakable, but yes, I checked the label just to be sure. Whiskey. I didn't misinterpret shit—your wonderful plant manager was drinking on the job. I did what I had to do, Matt. Exactly what you or dad would have done under the circumstances."

"Damn." He blew out a hard breath. "Did he at least try to explain himself?"

She shrugged. "He was clearly angry about something, not that it mattered. He was lit up like a Christmas tree and smashed a bottle against the door. If I'd walked in a second earlier, I'd be at the hospital right now getting stitches in my head. Which reminds me, I need to call Bernie and have maintenance—"

"There has to be some kind of reason for his behavior. His work record is impeccable. He ran the old plant like a well-oiled machine for over twenty years. Started when he was just out of high school, and worked his way up to operational manager by the time he was twenty eight."

"You seem to know a lot about this guy. It's almost as if you know him personally, like he's a friend or—"

"He's Drew's father."

Chapter Nine

"All right, Pop, you wanna tell me what's going on?"

Andrew Porter Sr. climbed hesitantly into the passenger side of Drew's pickup and leaned his head back, closing his eyes as if to shut out the world. Drew knew something major had to have happened for his father to have gotten himself fired.

He put the truck in park and waited for his old man to speak. When he didn't, Drew said, "Look, whatever it is, we can fix it. Lindy can be a little...intense at first. But once you get to know—"

"I opened that bottle of bourbon Kurt gave me for Christmas and drank...quite a bit of it. That's how Miss Spalding found me."

Drew was quiet for a moment as he processed that bit of info. His father wasn't much of a drinker, never had been. A couple of beers during a ball game or when bowling with the guys, but that was about it. "Why? Pop, what happened?"

Andy swiveled his head and met Drew's gaze. The misery Drew saw nearly took his breath. "Son, I have something to tell you. I...Jesus, I have no idea how to say the words."

Scared, Drew murmured, "Just say it. What the hell's going on?"

"It's your mother. She...Drew, I'm so sorry. Yesterday...your mother took her own life."

The hairs on the back of Drew's neck stood up as his father's words sank in. He struggled to suck air into his lungs as gut-wrenching sorrow filled his chest, stealing his breath. The text he'd received last night had been from Hannah reminding him of their mother's birthday, wanting to know if he'd remembered to send roses to the hospital, as they did every year.

He hadn't.

Christ, Hannah. She was going to take this so hard.

"But...when? How? I thought she was doing so much better since they'd started her on that new pill...?"

His father swiped a hand across his face; a sob escaped him. Drew pulled him into a bear hug and, surprisingly, the old man let him. Drew knew this was killing him. He'd never stopped loving her, never stopped hoping she'd be well enough to come home someday.

Andy gave Drew a pat on the back to let him know he was okay. He cleared his throat, wiped his eyes on his sleeve, and settled back against the headrest. "The new medicine seemed to be working. Your mother was happy; she was alert. She knew who I was when I called. But I guess the last few days she started cheeking her meds, tossing 'em in the trash. The doctor had no idea why, though that quack wouldn't know his ass from a hole in the ground."

Drew nodded in agreement, though he knew it wasn't the doctor's fault.

"Anyway, she managed to steal a bottle of something called Cyclobenz-something or other. Muscle relaxers. She swallowed the whole goddamned bottle, then hid in the closet. By the time the orderlies found her, it was too late."

Tears burned Drew's eyes. He'd loved his mother, but he'd also spent most of his life resenting her. She'd never been there for him growing up, or Hannah. And when she was there, she'd barely spared her kids a thought. If she wasn't sleeping off a bender, she was verbally abusing Drew and completely ignoring Hannah, her impressionable young daughter. Drew had known about her mental illness, but as a child, he hadn't understood it. Now, he just wished...well, he wished he could go back in time and make a few changes. For one, he wished he'd have visited her more often, called her more often.

"I'm really sorry, Pop."

"Me, too, kid. Your mother's been institutionalized for years, but I never lost hope. Until today." He let out a deep sigh and gave his eyes one last rub. "We'd best go tell Hannah."

Lindy stared at Matt in stunned silence, struggling to process the bitter irony of his pronouncement. "Drew's father?" she murmured, more to herself than to Matt. When the words finely sunk in, she demanded, "Why the hell didn't you tell me? My God, Matt, I just fired Drew's father!"

"No shit, Sherlock, isn't that what I said?"

Lindy leaned back in one of *Coffee To Chai For*'s new padded chairs and closed her eyes, pinching the bridge of her nose. She had no idea how she was supposed to feel about this bit of news. As angry as she was with Drew, as hurt as she might have been by his actions, she felt terrible with the knowledge she'd just put his father out of work. But what else could she have done under the circumstances? Nothing. She'd done exactly what anyone in her position would have done.

But would Drew understand? Or would he accuse her of firing his father to get back at him? She blew out a heartfelt sigh. "Well, there's nothing that can be done now. I was more than justified in firing him. Drew...well, if he doesn't understand, I'm sorry. I was simply doing my job."

"You can hire him back."

She gave her head a negative shake. "No, I can't."

"You're as stubborn as Dad, you know that?" Matt shook his head as he opened a bundle of magazines and fanned them out on one of the new book racks.

"Matt, I'm sorry, but you know I can't do that. If I'd been someone else, Bernie, or one of the other workers, we could be facing a huge lawsuit right now."

Matt was silent while he processed the truth of her words, frustration etching his brow.

Whether he liked it or not—whether she liked it or not—she'd done what she had to do. What dad would have expected her to do.

"I truly am sorry."

His gaze softened. "I know. I just worry about the ramifications. You're not exactly the easiest person to…get to know, and—"

"You were going to say 'like'."

"—I'm afraid because most people haven't gotten a chance to know you, they may snub you over firing Drew's dad."

Lindy had never much cared what people thought of her. Most made snap judgments because of the way she looked and the ridiculous stories they wrote about her in the tabloids, comparing her to another high profile blonde heiress who truly seemed to enjoy the attention of the paparazzi. So Lindy had learned it was simpler to play up the snob persona and let everyone think what they wanted, than put herself out there and risk heartache and rejection.

However, the people of Redemption had welcomed Matt into their small town with open arms. And because there was no one on earth she cared about more than her big brother, Lindy knew she had to make an effort. Put herself out there and allow these people to get to know the real Lindy, not the rich bitch tabloid sensation most were used to seeing.

"What if I were to throw a party?"

"Excuse me?"

"A housewarming slash Valentine's Day party. We'll invite everyone in Mayberry."

"A party."

"You're not going to start repeating everything I say again, are you?" She sighed. "Yes, a party. Why not?"

Matt cocked a brow at her before slicing his box cutter through the top of a cardboard box. "I'm just not sure anyone will want to come once word gets out you fired Drew's dad. He's an extremely well-liked and respected man in this town."

"Dammit, Matt, he was drinking right there in the office. He was so drunk he could barely stand. And he almost creamed me with a bottle!"

"I know, and believe me, I understand your position. I'm just saying, he must have had a damn good reason to—"

"Get smashed on the job?" Lindy gave a ladylike snort. "Why don't you give me a few examples, Matt. What, exactly, is a good excuse to drink on the job? And let's not forget, destruction of property, and nearly taking my head off with a glass bottle." She took a sip of her coffee, waiting for a reply that made sense. Really, okay, she got it. Andrew Porter was Drew and Hannah's father and basically a decent guy. But he'd screwed up big time, and that was on him, not—

Matt lifted a stack of books from the box, and Lindy's heart hammered triple time in her chest. The cover of her latest release, *Moonlit Seduction*, stared back at her in almost mocking salute. Holy shit, Matt was stocking her new book! Of course she never used an author photo on the back cover, but she also never expected any of her family members to get close enough to one to possibly make a connection. And what if Hannah accidentally opened her mouth?

Okay, Miss Worst Case Scenario, chill out. There's no reason Matt, or anyone else in this town, would make the connection. And Lindy was fairly certain she could trust Hannah to keep her word...though she did just fire the girl's father. "I need a huge slice of chocolate cake."

Matt glanced back at her and grinned. Chocolate cake was her drug of choice when feeling guilty, and he knew it. She usually gorged herself right after a shoe shopping trip.

"You're in luck. The bakery delivered one this morning." He held one of her books up and gave his head an 'I don't get it' shake.

Lindy inwardly grated.

"I can't believe people buy this crap. But hey, if it sells, great."

Carrie came up and snatched the book from Matt's hand. "Idiot. You know how much I love my romance novels." She glanced at Lindy. "I suppose you agree with Matt...?"

If you only knew. "I rarely agree with Matt. And I do indulge in the occasional novel."

"Romance?" Matt asked with a skeptical lilt to his voice.

"Yes, Mr. Foot Rub, romance. Really, it's a miracle Carrie puts up with you."

"I know, right?" Carrie handed the book back to Matt.

He slapped her ass with it. "You go wild over my foot rubs, babe, stop fronting."

"Stop fronting?" Carrie laughed. "What are you, fifteen? Lindy, I have cinnamon rolls to ice, so I'll talk to you later." Carrie gave Matt one last eye-roll before heading back to the kitchen.

"She's just saving face," Matt shared once Carrie was out of ear shot. "We're barely in the front door before she's all over me. The woman is insatiable."

For some reason, his self-satisfied smirk annoyed her. "I could've lived the rest of my life without that visual, thanks."

"My pleasure." He grinned. "Still want a slice of that cake?"

"I'm meeting Bernie for dinner later, so I think I'll save my calories for Nino's. I also have a party to plan." She pulled a face. "Back home I'd give Jenée a call, and like magic she'd put something amazing together in no time at all. I'm on my own here...unless you want to help?"

"Oh, no you don't. Party planner is where I draw the line."

"Come on, Matt, this means a lot to me." And it did.

"What? Since when? I thought you couldn't stand *Mayberry* and all its inhabitants."

"That's not true, I...I like all your friends. And I like Bernie. Oh, and Bev Donovan, she's a sweet lady. Her son isn't bad either."

"Okay, okay. I'll make sure the whole town shows up at your house next Friday night. You take care of the rest."

"Your generosity astounds me."

He laughed. "Hey, Nino's caters, and they have the best food in town. Why don't you talk to someone while you're there tonight?"

"Ooh, excellent idea, Matty." Back in L.A. her party fare would consist of every kind of sushi imaginable and lots of champagne. Somehow she didn't think the former would go over well with the Redemption crowd.

"Anything for my favorite sister."

Lindy laughed and grabbed her purse. "I'd be touched if I wasn't your only sister. By the way, my only dress requirement for the party is red. Everyone has to wear something red."

"Now *that* was delicious," Lindy purred after her last bite of sweetened ricotta-filled cannoli. The cinnamon and chocolate chips were such a delectable combination. She'd kill for another, but having been a fairly disciplined eater her whole life thanks to her health-conscious mother, Lindy found the will to resist temptation. But damn, it was hard.

"Aren't they the best?" Bernie agreed as she swiped the last bit of filling off her plate. "My nana used to make the most amazing cannoli, and these are even better than hers. Sorry, Nana." she added with a heavenward apology.

No sooner had they wiped their mouths than Nino appeared. "I hope you enjoyed the meal."

"Very much. Thank you. The best Italian food I've ever eaten stateside, and I mean that." The Chicken Vesuvio truly was the most delicious she'd ever tasted. Lindy would have to be careful or she could grow quite fat here in Redemption. Not that she'd be here long enough to test that theory.

"Excellent, excellent." He handed her the catering invoice he'd promised would be ready before she left. "Okay, I think I have everything you requested. Please look it over and let me know if I forgot anything."

Wow, she thought, making sure to mask her surprise, *what an impressive selection*. Sicilian caponata, bruschetta, prosciutto and melon, crostini al salmone, cocktail meatballs, eggplant parm, antipasto salad, assorted pizzas, assorted Italian pastries and cookies, tiramisu, cannoli. The last brought a smile to her face.

"Nino, this is wonderful." She dug a pen from her purse and signed the contract. "Please add whatever deposit you require to my bill."

"Normally, I ask for fifty percent."

"Sounds about right, thanks so much." She handed him back the contract.

"Absolutely my pleasure, Miss Spalding."

Once Nino walked away, Bernie lifted her brows. "You don't do things half-assed, do you?"

Nope, she never had. And this party was more important than any she'd hosted before. "What can I say? I love to throw parties."

Bernie smiled and took a leisurely sip of her wine. "I still can't believe what happened today with Andy. I knew something wasn't quite right with him, but I never dreamt he was in his office getting sloshed. It's just so unlike him. Andy's usually so easygoing."

Slightly uncomfortable by the change of subject, Lindy leaned back and blew out a silent breath. Andy, it seemed, had yet another fan. "I truly feel awful about what happened. But I had no choice, Bernie. I had to fire him."

"I know, it just…sucks."

Bernie's attention was suddenly drawn to the front of the restaurant. Curious, Lindy turned to see what had totally captivated her new friend. A uniformed police officer shook hands with Nino before he and another officer were escorted to a table.

Lindy smiled with genuine pleasure when she recognized Officer Michael Donovan. Tall, dark hair, bedroom brown eyes framed by surprisingly thick lashes, Mike Donovan was about as handsome as they came. And hey, what woman didn't like a man in uniform? Lindy knew exactly why Bernie couldn't drag her eyes away from him. She gave her new friend a gentle kick under the table.

A quick scowl was replaced by pinkened cheeks. "What?"

Lindy laughed. "He's a hottie. And I happen to know he's single."

Bernie cleared her throat before tilting her wineglass to her lips. She met Lindy's gaze for a brief second before feigning interest in the sleeve of her stylish sage blouse.

"Cat got your tongue?" Lindy teased, intrigued by Bernie's reaction to the sexy cop.

As if she couldn't help herself, Bernie cast Officer Donovan another quick glance. "He's...not my type."

"Oh. So you don't go for tall, dark and handsome?"

Bernie gave her an eye-roll before gulping down the rest of her wine.

"Wow, you really have it bad. So tell me, what's the problem? You told me you were single."

"I *am* single. And I plan to stay that way, thank you very much." She motioned with her empty wineglass to the waitress.

"You're a little young to be so cynical, aren't you?" *Now isn't that the pot calling the kettle black*. Though Lindy wanted to find love, she truly did. It just hadn't happened yet.

Had it?

"Look, I know you mean well, but I'm just not interested in pursuing a relationship, or anything else, right now. With anyone."

Taken aback by the pain simmering behind those expressive amber eyes, Lindy apologized. "I'm sorry. We barely know each other, and here I am trying to take charge of your love life. As of this second, the subject is closed."

The waitress arrived with a second glass of wine for Bernie. "Can I bring you ladies anything else?" She picked up the empty dessert plates while waiting for a reply.

"I'm good," Lindy said.

"This'll do it for me, too. Thanks."

"Before I forget," Lindy added, "Nino is going to add a catering deposit to the bill. I don't know if he mentioned it or not."

"He did, and it's already on there." She pulled the bill from her pocket and placed it face down on the table beside Lindy.

"Thank you."

The waitress amped up her thousand watt tip making smile. "You're welcome. Just let me know when you're ready for me to take it up for you."

Lindy eyed Bernie as she dug her wallet out of her purse, somewhat concerned by the desolation in her new friend's eyes. "Probably best if we call it a night. I had a hell of a day and could really use a hot bath right about now."

Bernie seemed to perk up at that. "You and me both. Listen, I'm sorry for becoming such a downer."

"You don't have to apologize. I was a bit pushy."

"No, you asked a perfectly normal question, and I freaked."

Curious, Lindy wanted to question Bernie further. But they barely knew each other and she didn't want to risk pushing her new friend away.

After one last sip of her wine, Bernie hooked her hobo bag purse over her shoulder, and rose to her feet. "Thanks again for dinner, Lindy. Can I at least leave the tip?"

"Not a chance. Dinner is on me, period." Lindy smiled, having enjoyed the evening more than she'd expected to. Bernie was as sophisticated as any of her friends back home, with the added bonus of being side-splittingly funny.

"Okay, but next time, it's on me. Please."

"Deal."

Lindy finished her wine, paid the bill, and headed out. An icy blast of wind tore the door from her hand and slapped her in the face, nearly stealing her breath. She grasped the lapels of her jacket with one hand and clenched them under her chin. This freezing cold weather was something she'd never get used to. Not that she'd have to. Regardless of why Drew raced out of her bedroom last night, firing his father was most definitely the icing on the 'it's over before it began' cake.

In serious need of that hot bath, Lindy decided to skip stopping back at *Coffee To Chai For* to tell Matt about the menu. Shivering, she dug out her cell phone and gave him a call. It went straight to voicemail. "Hey, don't forget to invite Beverly Donovan and her son, Officer Mike Donovan, to the party. And Matty, you were right. You wouldn't believe the incredible menu Nino put together for me. Thanks again."

Binks meowed a greeting the moment Lindy stuck her key in the lock and followed along as Lindy climbed the two flights of stairs to her bedroom—no doubt hoping for a belly rub. Lindy started the water running, adding a few capfuls of vanilla-scented bubble bath before slipping off her clothes and twisting her hair up in a clip. She grabbed the romantic comedy she'd picked up at the grocery store and sank down into the steaming water with a deep sigh of contentment.

And of course that's when someone decided to pound on her front door.

Chapter Ten

"What the hell am I doing here?" Drew muttered as he stared at Lindy's front door.

He'd had a few beers, brooded over his father's firing, grieved for the mother he'd never really known. Hannah had taken the news in the same stoic manner he'd expected, then quietly cried her heart out in the sanctuary of her bedroom. It about killed him to hear her muffled sobs, wanting to go in and comfort her, yet in too volatile a frame of mind to trust himself. Christ, he couldn't even comfort his baby sister during the worst time of their lives.

Love, hate, anger, sadness—Drew's emotions had been running the gamut for hours. Though he'd yet to shed a tear, he'd never felt more physically drained, as if he'd just finished the Ironman Triathlon. But also oddly restless; unable to sit for more than two minutes at a time, incapable of doing anything constructive, like work on Hannah's car. Finally, he'd given up on finding any kind of peace, and hopped in his truck. He'd known exactly where he was heading before he'd even crammed the key in the ignition.

Come on, woman, answer the friggin' door. Hunching his shoulders against the bitter cold, Drew's irritation bubbled into a full, roiling boil. Her car was in the driveway, so she had to be home. If she'd already gone to bed, too damn bad. They needed to talk—now. Fairly busting at the seams with repressed fury, Drew needed to vent.

And the only other person who deserved his wrath was lying in a morgue.

Driven by a truckload of warring emotions, Drew pounded again, the last of his patience dissipating into the frigid night air. Still no answer. He tried the knob—locked. Then he remembered he still had a key to the place. For some reason he kept forgetting to return it.

Or maybe it was fate.

Before he could talk himself out of it, Drew stuck the key in the lock and opened the door.

"What the hell do you think you're doing?"

Drew looked up, and there stood Miss High and Mighty, glaring down at him in disapproval—and looking so beautiful it should be a crime. His jaw clenched; he shut the door behind him and relocked it. She wore a silky blue bathrobe with her hair pinned loosely on top of her head, looking as if she were about to step into a hot bath. The thought caused an uncomfortable ache in his groin, which only kicked his frustration up a notch. Damn it, he didn't want to desire the merciless bitch, whose heart was as wintry as the ice-blue of her robe.

But desire her he did. Blood surged hot through his veins; every inch of him throbbed with longing. He'd wanted this woman from the moment she'd fish-tailed into his life, and he was damn tired of denying himself. Tunnel vision thrust every other thought from his head as he shed his leather jacket and tossed it, with his keys, onto the chair. *Mine*, some primeval voice thundered in his head, propelling him forward as if by physical force.

"Look, I-I know why you're here, but we have nothing to talk about. I was perfectly justified in firing your father. He...hey, you stop right there!"

Spurred by a combination of pounding lust and an unidentifiable emotion he was loathe to examine, Drew started up the stairs, his steps quickening as raw hunger took control of his senses. He needed the headstrong woman more than he needed air at that moment, and he knew, despite protest, she wanted him just as much. When Lindy turned and raced up the stairs, Drew gave chase without a second thought.

He caught her by the arm just as she reached her bedroom. She spun around and swung with her free hand, slapping his face with a resounding whack. Drew caught her arm before she could swing again and yanked her flush against his chest. Her hair clip fell to the floor; Drew slid one hand into the silky blonde mane, his eyes centered on her delectable mouth. Chests heaved as they glared at each other—she in angry defiance, he in agonizing need.

"You want me." The harsh rasp of his voice surprised him.

"I don't!" Her protest was in direct contrast with her roaming hands, which had twined around his neck.

A triumphant smile chased away his irritation, his own hands kneading the gentle swell of her hips. "Liar."

Her defenses crumbled as anger turned to uncertainty. "You...you walked out on me last night."

"You were tipsy. I didn't want to take advantage." Okay, only a half truth. If Hannah hadn't sent him that voice mail, he couldn't swear his inner moral compass would have led him in the right direction.

He gently traced the shell of her ear with his fingertips, then the line of her jaw, the curve of her delicate throat. She closed her eyes, concealing her emotions as effectually as if she'd donned a mask. Her head lolled back, allowing him the access he craved.

Drew didn't waste a second, following the path of his fingers with his lips, drawing an answering shudder from her. His lips sought hers, exploring leisurely at first, savoring her taste, her softness, then deepening the kiss, plumbing the moist recesses of her delectable mouth. Her arms tightened around his neck as she eagerly met the thrust of his tongue, blowing his mind with her fervent response.

Slipping an arm beneath her legs, he picked her up and carried her to the bed. They fell in a tangle of limbs, hungry lips never breaking contact. Lindy surprised him with her assertiveness, quickly stripping him of his T-shirt before grasping the button of his jeans. Jesus, at this rate he'd embarrass himself before she even got his zipper down.

He broke off the kiss, desperate to get himself under control. Seemed like he'd waited for this woman forever, and the last thing he wanted to do was disappoint. Call it plain old male pride, but tonight he planned to ruin little Miss Hot Stuff for other men.

A flash of uncertainty lit her gaze. He reassured her by kicking off his boots, toeing off his socks, and shucking his jeans. When that sexy siren's smile returned, Drew slipped his thumbs beneath the elastic of his boxer briefs and slipped them off.

Satisfaction shone in the slight widening of those liquid brown pools. She rose to her knees, untied the sash of her robe, and spread it open, revealing utter perfection beneath. Rock-hard and aching, Drew knelt before her on the bed and drank in his fill. Flawless was the only word that came to mind. The woman was simply flawless.

They came together without pretense, lips melding in wild abandonment, restless hands stroking, squeezing, wanting. Drew had never needed anyone more than he did the beautiful woman in his arms. He cupped her breasts, kneading the soft globes with near reverence before teasing the luscious pink tips into pebbled peaks. Her sexy little moans drove him wild, and it was all he could do to keep from tossing her back and sinking into her welcoming heat.

She caressed a fiery trail up the hard planes of his back, over his shoulders, tracing her fingers down his chest and stomach with slow appreciation until they curled eagerly around the proof of his desire. She met his gaze, her own heavy with desire.

"God *yes*," he muttered, his voice thick, as he turned to stone in her hand.

She leaned in and nipped at his lower lip while slowly stroking his shaft in her tight fist. Drew reclaimed her lips, grasping her ass with one hand while palming the back of her head with the other, holding her steady as he plundered her hot mouth. She met his tongue eagerly, impatiently, as hungry for their coming together as he was. Hell, his heart was pounding as if he were getting laid for the first time!

Stunned—and a little damn scared—to discover just how strongly her touch affected him, he hooked a hand under her knee and gently coaxed her down on the bed, desperate to regain some semblance of control.

And do a little exploring of his own.

She released him and sank back into the downy comforter, watching through the thick fringe of her lashes. He lowered his mouth to one succulent nipple, laving it with his tongue, teasing it with his teeth before bestowing the same loving attention to its twin. Her taste, her intoxicating scent...Drew couldn't get enough of her. Lindy arched into him, her body silently begging him for more.

He smoothed one hand down the silken skin of her belly, through the golden curls guarding her plump folds, until his fingers sank into her slick passage. She exhaled sharply, as if surprised by the invasion, then relaxed, wrapping one leg around his thigh, urging him on in silent plea. He'd wanted to take his time, fly her to the moon and back before taking his own pleasure, but Lindy's passionate response was stripping away what little self-control he had.

She reached between them and wrapped her fingers around his cock, nuzzling his neck as she guided him between her thighs. "Please," she murmured against his throat. "I need you inside me."

He hardened like steel at her whispered pronouncement. The tenuous hold he had on his self-restraint dissipated. With a guttural curse, Drew grasped her under one knee, and slid home with one smooth stroke.

They became one hard and fast, lips seeking and meshing, his forearms cradling her from beneath. Lindy's arms wrapped around his back, her calves wrapped around his thighs as they surged together in a mutual rush of sexual need, bodies straining, mingled groans of pleasure growing louder and deeper with each desperate thrust. With a hoarse shout and a soft cry of release, they rode a wave of pure ecstasy right over the edge into oblivion.

Holy shit, Drew thought as he labored for breath, his heart pounding a furious staccato against his ribcage. Once their breathing slowed, he rolled them over, and crushed Lindy in his embrace. He'd been with his fair share of women, but none had ever made him feel as alive as he felt at that moment. Drew held her tight, hoping the satisfied smile on his face wasn't too pathetic. But damn, did he feel good.

"Wow."

Drew chuckled and pressed his lips to her temple. "My thoughts exactly."

Not quite ready to look him in the eye, Lindy savored the bliss of merely lying in his arms. And the man did have some nice arms. *Heck, he has nice everything*, she thought, happier at that moment than she'd ever thought possible.

She reveled in the knowledge that he'd left the night before *not* because he didn't want her, but because he was honorable. Honorable *and* an amazing lover. The thought sent a warm flush from the top of her head to the tips of her toes. And muscular. The man was strong as an ox—something that had always been a huge turn-on for her. She'd felt the strength pulsing through him as he'd driven her to heaven and beyond. And he smelled incredible; spicy and masculine and...a small sigh escaped her and she bit her lip to hold back a grin.

Yep, Melinda Sue Spalding was dangerously close to falling in love. And the biggest surprise? The thought didn't scare her nearly as much as it should.

Her smile faded as reality struck. She'd be heading back to L.A. once the plant was up and running. Though Redemption and its inhabitants were slowly worming their way into her heart, could she imagine a life here permanently? And what about her parents?

They'd be heartbroken if she moved so far away from them.

Though Matt was here. Maybe if both their kids were living in Redemption, Mom and Dad would make the move as well. The L.A. Spaldings living in Middle America. Now there was an idea for a reality show if she'd ever heard one.

"I've just watched a million expressions cross your face. Should I be concerned?"

Lindy laughed and plucked at his chest hair, which was just as sexy as the rest of him. A T of golden perfection that narrowed down his stomach and disappeared beneath the covers. "No, I was just thinking."

"That's what worries me," he teased, tightening his hold. "You think too much."

"Can't argue with you there. Though I'm pretty content right now." Her thoughts worked around to the reason she suspected he'd landed on her step in the first place. "Maybe we should talk about your father."

Drew blew out a deep breath, then extricated himself from her arms and lay back on the pillow, linking his fingers behind his head. Probably would've been a better idea to save this particular conversation, but she saw no point in putting off the inevitable.

"I'd like to try and explain his actions, if you'll let me."

Missing the comfort of his embrace, Lindy rolled onto her side and propped her head on her palm. "I really am sorry about what happened, but—"

"But you were only doing your job," he finished, turning slightly to meet her gaze. "I know. He explained the entire scene to me, and anyone in your position would've done the same thing. I get it. I just want you to know the truth, what it was that set him off like that. My old man isn't a drunk or a violent man. He's one of the most even-tempered, clear-headed people you'll ever meet."

She placed her hand on his chest, over his heart. "Tell me."

Drew cleared his throat, and then explained about his mother's mental illness, how she'd spent more time drinking and running around than with her impressionable young children. Despite everything, Drew's father had adored his wife, and though they'd finally had to institutionalize her, he'd never stopped loving her, never stopped believing she'd be well enough someday to come home. And they'd never divorced; his father having stayed faithful to her all these years.

How heartbreaking, Lindy thought. She and Matt had been blessed with wonderful parents, so she couldn't imagine what Drew and Hannah's childhood must have been like. Lindy laid her head on Drew's chest and snuggled into his embrace. His arms closed around her with a reassuring squeeze, as if *he* were trying to comfort *her*.

"Yesterday morning," Drew continued, "dad got a call from the hospital. My mother had taken a whole bottle of muscle relaxers sometime the night before. By the time they found her, it was too late."

Stunned, she whispered, "My God...Drew, I'm so sorry."

He stroked her hair with a gentle hand. "Dad took it hard. He had a bottle of brandy in his desk at work. Unopened; it was a Christmas gift from a friend. And since he rarely drinks the hard stuff, it hit him like a ton of bricks. He'd completely forgotten he was supposed to meet with you. He feels awful. Wanted me to make sure you weren't hurt."

"I'm fine," she said in a soft voice, touched the man even thought to ask about her with all that had happened.

Drew grew quiet suddenly, gazing down at her with an intensity that nearly stole her breath.

She recognized the look, and her body responded as he rolled them over, pinning her beneath him. He captured her mouth with passionate need, craving the same comfort she sought from him.

They made love again, slowly this time, savoring each touch, each caress. Lindy ached for him in ways she'd never before experienced. Until Drew, no man had ever made it past her defenses, had ever evoked such a passionate response from her, and she reveled in her newfound sexual freedom. She'd given him a rough time of it from day one, but he'd given it back ten-fold. Drew was her match in every way, and Lindy thrilled at the possibility of a future with him.

As their bodies cooled, Drew pulled her tight against his chest, spoon-style. She closed her eyes with a sigh of pure contentment, exhausted and blissfully happy. She'd have a lot of thinking to do after tonight, that was for sure.

He nipped at her ear, then whispered, "You're amazing, you know that?"

"You're pretty awesome yourself, *Lou,*" she teased, her cheeks sore from smiling. Had she ever smiled so much in her life?

He gave her ass a slap. "Sassy witch. I think you need a spanking."

"Somehow, that doesn't sound like punishment."

Drew laughed and gave her another playful swat. After a moment, he asked, "So how long until the plant's up and running?"

"We plan to open the doors on May 1st, and thankfully, we're right on schedule." Then it's back to L.A. and civilization. At least until she could sell her condo and race back to Mayberry. The thought didn't cause her even a single quiver of concern. In fact, her writing had come alive since arriving, the words flowing like they never had before.

She wasn't sure if it was her imagination, or if she was looking too much into it, but Drew stiffened and withdrew from her a bit. Regrets? Already? God, she hoped not. Not when she'd all but made the decision to relocate here. No...no, she was being paranoid. She'd just had the most incredible sex of her life—twice. No way could he not be feeling what she was feeling.

Could it be about his father? Had Drew expected her to offer the man his job back just because they'd slept together? The thought that Drew could have very well assumed just that brought an uncomfortable ache to her chest.

He sat up and swiped both hands through his hair. He looked haggard, suddenly, and she wondered if he was thinking about his mother. Of course, that had to be it. She could only imagine what hell the man was going through, not to mention the burden of worrying about his father and sister on top of dealing with his own grief.

He threw the covers back and sat on the edge of the bed for a moment, as if collecting his thoughts, then picked his boxer briefs off the floor and slipped them on. Lindy snuggled back against the pillows and watched him shrug into his shirt though sated eyes. The man had the body of a Greek God; anticipation thrummed through her as she imagined the next time she'd have him naked in her bed.

Fully dressed, he turned, but barely looked her in the eye as he said, "It's been fun, Hot Stuff, but I have to get going. Lots to do tomorrow."

It's been fun? "I don't understand. Is something wrong?" When he didn't immediately respond, her pulse sped up. "Drew?"

His eyes narrowed, grew cold; distant. "Don't you mean *Lou*?"

"I was kidding." She frowned. "You know that."

He blew out another hard breath and scrubbed a hand over his face. "Yeah, you were kidding. Listen, seriously, I have to go. We'll talk later." With that, Drew took off as if his feet were on fire, slamming the front door on his way out.

Lindy wrapped her arms around herself, tears burning her eyes, and gazed unseeingly out her bedroom window. This had to be about his grief over his mother. Maybe something she'd said reminded him of her. Or maybe in his vulnerable state the solace of her arms wasn't the only comfort he needed. Maybe tonight he needed to grieve with his family.

And crap, she'd completely forgotten to mention the party. Not that he or Hannah would be in a celebratory mood anytime soon. But it wasn't for another ten days, so hopefully they'd feel up to it by then. In the meantime, she would have some faith and do something she'd never done before in her life. Give Drew his space and wait for him to call.

Chapter Eleven

━━━━━━━✧━━━━━━━

 $\mathcal{L}$ indy had just washed down the last bite of
her burger down when Hannah entered the
diner. The younger girl hung her coat and
tucked her purse away, apparently about to start
her shift. Lindy hoped she'd come over and say
hello before she did since Lindy hadn't had a
chance yet to offer her condolences. Also, Drew
hadn't called since the night they'd made love,
and while Lindy understood he had a lot going
on right now, she couldn't help but worry.

 Hannah spoke with Hutch for a moment
before turning to face her. The despair in her
eyes put Lindy on edge. God, she hoped
nothing else had happened in the last few
days.

When Hannah reached her table, Lindy stood up and wrapped her arms around her. "I'm so sorry about your mother. If there's anything I can do for you, please let me know."

"Thanks, Lindy. I appreciate that."

Lindy sat back down and gestured for Hannah to join her. "Just for a minute."

With a reluctant nod, Hannah sat down across from her.

"I haven't heard from Drew in several days and…well, I wanted to make sure he was all right…?"

A flare of surprise lit Hannah's eyes. "I'm really sorry, but…I assumed you knew. Drew decided to stay in Michigan after the funeral."

"For how long?"

"Indefinitely."

Stunned, Lindy could only stare at Hannah. Stay in Michigan indefinitely? She had to have heard her wrong. "I don't understand. He has a business to run. He…"

He what? He was madly in love with her? Ready to build a life with her? The only thing she knew for sure was they'd had mind-blowing sex—twice—then he ran off as soon as the sheets cooled. In fact, he ran out on her a lot. The man owed her an explanation if nothing else, though she was starting to doubt she'd get one.

Pity swam in Hannah's gaze. Talk about humiliating.

"I wish I knew what to tell you. When I asked him what was going on, he said it was nothing. I sort of assumed you two had gotten into an argument or something."

Yeah, or something.

Willing herself not to tear up, Lindy changed the subject. "I need to speak with your father. Any chance I might be able to catch him at home?"

The question brought a smile of relief to Hannah's face. "He just dropped me off, so he should be home any minute."

"Thanks. Hey, did Matt happen to mention the party I'm throwing next Friday? I hope you can make it."

"I'll definitely try. Sounds like a blast."

When Lindy arrived at Drew's house, she sat in the car for a moment, more than a little anxious to face the elder Mr. Porter again. She planned to offer him his job back, and sincerely hoped he would accept. What had happened was unfortunate, but she had a lot of sympathy for the man now that she knew the whole story, and was willing to scratch the incident from the record for a fresh start.

And her decision had nothing whatsoever to do with sleeping with his son. After thinking about it from every angle, Lindy knew even her hard-nosed father would agree—Andrew Porter deserved a second chance.

Her thoughts collected, Lindy got out of the car and crossed the street, taking a deep, calming breath before rapping on the door. The night had grown bitterly cold, and she became engrossed in the way the moonlight glinted off the icicles hanging from the gutter above her head as she waited for him to answer the door. Nervous energy started her toe tapping and her head bopping from side to side as she softly hummed the theme song to her favorite sitcom.

The door swung open, taking her by surprise. Andrew Porter squinted in confusion for a moment before recognition dawned. A hesitant smile quirked his lips. "Miss Spalding. I wasn't expecting you...was I?"

Lindy laughed, though the sound was born of awkwardness. "No, and I'm sorry to bother you at home. I was hoping we could talk."

With a cautious nod, Andrew stepped back to allow her inside. He closed the door behind her and motioned her into the kitchen. "I just put on a pot of coffee. Would you like a cup?"

"I'd love one, thank you." She glanced around, careful not to appear too nosey. Naturally, she had a healthy curiosity about the

Porter clan. From the father, who'd loved his wife so much he'd never given up hope, even when faced with mental illness, to the daughter, who'd accidentally stumbled upon Lindy's deepest secret, to the son, who despite the intimacy they'd shared was still such a mystery.

"There's cream and sugar on the Lazy Susan," he said as he set a steaming mug and a spoon on the table. "Please, sit."

With a nod, Lindy set her purse on the chair beside her and sat. She took her time stirring powdered creamer and sugar into her mug while she contemplated the easiest way to get to the point.

"I'm, uh, glad you stopped by," he said after a moment. "I've been wanting to apologize for my behavior the other day. I'm completely mortified and sorrier than I can say. I'm just relieved you weren't hurt."

"Drew explained what happened. I'm so sorry for your loss."

Andrew pressed his lips together and finally sat down across from her.

They sipped their coffee in quiet contemplation until the silence became deafening. Finally, Lindy came to the point. "I'd like to offer you your job back. I have it on good authority that you're the best plant manager in the Midwest, and I'd be a fool to try and replace you."

He fingered the rim of his mug, a small smile chasing away his mournful grimace. "Matt's been singing my praises, hey?"

"And then some."

He laughed. "I'm pretty fond of him myself."

"So?"

Andrew held out his hand and she grasped it. "I know I don't deserve a second chance, but I'm truly grateful for it, so thank you. I swear you won't regret it."

"I have no doubt that's true." When she would've let go, he clung to her hand, his expression shifting, growing more thoughtful.

"I don't want to stick my nose into your business. But I know you and my son...well, I know there's something there. I need to explain a few things to you so you'll understand."

Lindy's pulse sped up at this unexpected turn of conversation. "Understand what?"

"My son."

"No disrespect, Mr. Porter," she slipped her hand from his, "but I think I know everything I need to know about your son."

"I'm fairly certain he's in love with you, though I doubt he's ready to admit it. To you or himself."

Swallowing down the flare of hope his pronouncement ignited, Lindy gave a negative shake of her head. "I'm sorry, but you're mistaken. Drew couldn't get away from me fast enough the other..." Her cheeks flamed when she realized what she'd been about to admit. She instantly became annoyed with herself. She and Drew were both consenting adults and—

"I won't pretend to know what happened between the two of you. However, I *do* know my son, and I've never seen him so twisted up over a woman before. It's a new experience for him, trust me on that."

Trust was not a word she could easily associate with Drew Porter. Unreliable, yes. Indecisive, absolutely. But trustworthy? Hardly. After the way he'd run out on her, not to mention his decision to stay away "indefinitely", how could she trust anything when it came to that man?

"He seemed pretty clear about what he wanted when he...when he walked out on me."

There, she'd said it; admitted aloud just how hurt she'd been by Drew's disappearance. She also realized how desperately she wanted his father to assure her of Drew's love and his intention of returning home. Hopefully, before she had to head back to L.A. To either put her condo up for sale and break the news of her relocation to her parents, or settle back into life in the city and forget about the only man who'd ever made her feel…anything.

"Drew took his mother's abandonment hard," Andrew quietly explained. "She loved her children, she truly did. But she was sick. Some days she'd hug him tight, whisper how much she loved him. Others he couldn't do anything right. If she wasn't ranting and raving about some small infraction, she ignored him completely. To say he grew up with a confused sense of what motherly love is would be an understatement."

"I don't know what to say. I can't even imagine…those poor kids."

Staring off into the past, he gave a sad nod of agreement. "Hannah's several years younger than Drew, so thankfully she was spared most of the mind games. Drew wasn't so lucky. He's as cynical as the day is long when it comes to women. Frankly, I never expected that to change." He met her gaze. "But then we were getting a sandwich at Hutch's about a week back, and some punk made a crude comment about you. Drew told him if he so much as spoke your name again, he'd bust his jaw." Andrew chuckled. "I think mine about hit the floor."

"Mr. Porter—"

"Andrew. Please."

She nodded. "Andrew, I...I like Drew. A lot. But I think you may be reading too much into this. The strongest feeling Drew's ever felt for me is major frustration."

That brought a smile to the older man's face. "Oh, I have no doubt of that. Though not for the reasons you think." He gave her a little wink, then took a healthy gulp of his coffee.

"You know something? You're every bit as infuriating as your son."

Masculine laughter filled the room as new hope blossomed in Lindy's heart. Now if the stubborn man would only show up at her party so she could show him how much he—and this town—had come to mean to her.

Lindy had been checking the weather channel all week, and until this morning the forecast included some light flurries and temps in the low thirties. But of course, the day her party arrived, the light flurries were upgraded to a winter storm warning. Thankfully, the heavy snow wouldn't arrive until after midnight, so after talking to Matt and Carrie, she decided to go forward with the party.

A couple of hours before the guests were due to arrive, freshly showered and dressed in her comfy sweats, Lindy took a quick sweep through the house to make sure she hadn't forgotten anything. Nino's crew of ten had just started setting up the buffet tables, which lined three walls in the dining room and continued on into the hall.

Wow, she'd forgotten just how much food and drink she'd ordered. But since the champagne would be flowing, she'd wanted to make sure everyone had plenty to eat. Hopefully, Nino had thought to bring along take-home boxes for any leftovers.

"Miss Spalding?" he called from the kitchen.

She made her way in, smiling at the beautiful décor. The entire first floor had been swathed in red, white, and pink roses, carnations, and calla lilies. Lindy had had to pay a fortune for so many fresh flowers, but to her the cost had been worth it. Her home looked absolutely breathtaking. And the sweet floral fragrance wafting through the air was intoxicating.

"Call me Lindy, please," she said, making a mental note to put out the dishes of red and white M&Ms and Hershey's Kisses before she ran upstairs to get dressed. It was the little details that made a party a success, and Lindy was anal about the details.

He smiled, taking her hand as she approached. "The pizzas will be delivered at seven o'clock; everything else is being prepped here."

"Perfect. Thank you so much." With a delighted smile, she squeezed Nino's hand and marveled once again over the beauty around her before hurrying upstairs to her room. She'd never been this excited about a party before. It truly meant something, and she had no trouble admitting that anymore. Plus, the sizzling red dress she'd chosen for tonight was most definitely going to knock a certain auto mechanic's socks off.

If he showed up. Matt had spoken to Charlie a few nights ago, who'd filled Drew in on the party. Guess she'd just have to wait and see...though she wouldn't hold her breath.

Lindy twisted her hair up in a loose chignon with a curled tendril sweeping down the left side of her face. She didn't apply much makeup, though she did go a little heavy on mascara and the cherry red lipstick she'd purchased specifically for the party. The only jewelry she wore dangled from ears; the heart-shaped diamond earrings had been a gift from her father last Valentine's Day. The strapless silk dress she wore was simple yet elegant, and she paired it with the shiny red patent Manolo's she'd picked up last summer in New York.

A plethora of delicious aromas began to make their way upstairs. Lindy glanced at the clock, stunned to realize it was already quarter to six. Her guests should start arriving any minute. After one last glance in the mirror, she sucked in a deep breath, blew it out slowly, and then hustled down the stairs.

Anticipation hummed in her veins as she envisioned everyone's surprise when they stepped inside the foyer and experienced the floral paradise she'd created—with lots of help from Bernie, who had become a great friend in such a short time. If things didn't work out and Lindy headed back to L.A., she'd miss the vivacious brunette.

Stop it, she chided herself. *No pessimistic thinking allowed tonight.*

The doorbell rang, pulling her from her unpleasant musings. Her first guest had arrived! Lord, you'd think this was the first party she'd thrown. Laughing at herself, Lindy opened the door with a flourish and batted her eyelashes at her brother and Carrie.

Bernie stood beside them, beaming. "Ready?"

"I'm always ready," Lindy countered, stepping back to allow them inside.

Carrie gasped as she took in the red, white, and pink wonderland around her. "Holy Moly, woman, you really went all out." Her gaze settled on Lindy, then shifted to Bernie, who'd just slipped off her coat to reveal the red satiny pantsuit beneath. Carrie gave a rueful lift of one brow. "I'm starting to think I'm underdressed."

Preening, Lindy did a graceful spin. "How do I look?"

"Ridiculously gorgeous," Carrie drawled. "You, too," she added with a sidelong glance at Bernie. She shucked her Packers stadium jacket and looked down at her red, cashmere cowl neck sweater, black jeans, and red sneakers.

Lindy gestured for Matt to take the ladies' coats. "You can hang them in the hall closet. Carrie, I think you look absolutely wonderful. The shoes are a perfect touch. Bernie— stunning." Lindy's smile drooped as Matt shrugged out of his own Packers jacket. He wore jeans, with a red pocket T-shirt. "Really? That's all you could come up with?"

"What? You said red." He plucked at his shirt. "This is red."

She rolled her eyes. Small town living had been good for Matt in a lot of ways, but not when it came to his sense of style. In less than a year, Mr. GQ had transformed into Mr. Country Living.

Bernie hooked her arm through Lindy's. "So where's the bubbly?"

Within an hour, it seemed as if half of Redemption filled her home, and Lindy was absolutely thrilled by the turnout. She gloried in her role as party hostess, greeting all new guests personally, making sure everyone had food and drink. Nino's delicious Italian cuisine disappeared from the trays as fast as the servers put it out, and the champagne flowed freely. Everyone 'oohed' and 'ahhed' as soon as they walked in the door, which pleased Lindy to no end. The field she'd had snow-plowed across the street already had so many vehicles it looked like the parking lot at a Lakers game.

Nino, his wife, and their son, Nico, arrived with the freshly-made pizzas, much to everyone's delight. She had to admit, the casual, friendly atmosphere of her small town get-together was so much more enjoyable than any L.A. bash she'd ever attended. Or thrown. And as much as Lindy loved a good party, that was saying something.

Only one thing could make this night perfect, though she'd started to give up hope he'd show up.

Bernie ran up with panic-filled eyes and grabbed Lindy by the arm. "Mike's here! I'm pretty sure that's his truck that just pulled up."

"Oh, good. I was hoping he'd make it."

"You invited him?"

"Well, technically Matt invited him, but I asked him to. Why? Does his presence here make you uncomfortable?" A knowing grin accompanied Lindy's question. A knock on the door confirmed Mike's arrival.

Bernie propped her hands on her hips and lifted her chin. "Sneaky shit."

Lindy laughed. "Come on, I couldn't very well invite all of Redemption *except* for Officer Donovan. How would that have looked?" Without waiting for a reply, Lindy swung the door open. Only it wasn't Mike standing on her front porch, but Charlie's friend, Allie. The dog sitter dating that cute veterinarian. With her back to the door, Allie stared off into the distance as if lost in thought.

"Allie? Would you like to come in?"

She spun around. "Hey, Lindy. Beautiful house."

"Thank you. Wait'll you see the inside." Lindy stepped aside to allow her entrance, noting she didn't have a drop of red on. Not that it mattered. Allie looked as if she had more important things on her mind. "Is Rick parking the truck?"

Ignoring the question, Allie stepped inside the foyer and gazed around. Though genuine appreciation lit her eyes, she didn't comment. Instead, she asked, "Have you seen Dana?"

"Check the library, just off the formal dining room. I'm pretty sure she and Charlie headed that way."

Allie attempted a smile, though it didn't quite reach her eyes. "Thanks," she murmured before hurrying off in search of her friends.

The girl was definitely preoccupied, and it hadn't escaped her that Allie never replied about Rick. Trouble in paradise? Before Lindy could dwell on it, there was a knock at the door. Now this must be Officer Donovan. Lindy threw the door back open and smiled up at the handsome cop, who was flanked by Carrie's brother, fellow officer Chase Lowell.

"Well, hello officers," she purred, inviting them in with a crook of her finger. "I'm so glad you both could make it."

"Champagne and Nino's? I can't think of a better incentive to wear red," Chase teased. Lindy gave his red tie a playful tug.

"Thanks for the invite," Mike added. He gave her an appreciative once over. "You look amazing."

"Why thank you, kind sir." She playfully batted her eyelashes before looping her arm through his. "Come on, boys, food and champagne are this way."

She waited until Mike and Chase had each grabbed a glass of champagne and a couple slices of pizza, then directed them to the library where she knew most of that particular crowd had congregated. She was about to run back upstairs to check her make up when she caught Allie out of the corner of her eye, who appeared to be even more distraught than when she'd arrived. Lindy watched as Dana put an arm around her friend's shoulders and steered her through the mob of people out into the hall, Charlie's sister, Tara, on their heels. Dana led them into the small bedroom next door.

Concerned, Lindy followed along and poked her head inside. "Is everything okay?"

"I'm not pregnant," Allie wailed before dissolving into tears.

Lindy's heart broke for Allie, who obviously wasn't happy with her pronouncement.

"Okay." Dana shot a surprised look up at Tara before asking, "Shouldn't that be a good thing?"

Allie shook her head. "Rick asked me to marry him."

Lindy's respect for the handsome vet grew. She pressed a hand to her stomach as the sudden realization that she herself could be pregnant registered. She and Drew hadn't used protection either time, and crap...she was right in the middle of her cycle. If indeed she was, would Drew offer to marry her? Would she even want to marry the impossible man?

"What'd you say?" Dana asked Allie.

"I said yes, but only because I thought I was pregnant. And I think he only asked because he thought I was pregnant."

"But you're not."

Tears streamed down Allie's face. "No."

Lindy grabbed a box of tissues off the nightstand and pressed a handful into Allie's hands.

Dana frowned at Allie. "So, what, doesn't he want to get married now?"

"He said it doesn't change things."

"Then I don't understand what the problem is."

Allie blew her nose, looked from Dana, up at Tara and Lindy, then back down to her hands where she shredded one of the tissues. She reached up to tuck her hair behind her ear. "I have a medical condition, and I'll probably never be able to have kids."

Tears sprang to Lindy's eyes. Poor Allie. She clearly wanted children very much, but because of the luck of the genetic draw, she may not be able to have any. Lindy couldn't even imagine, especially now that she'd realized how much she wanted children of her own. Guilt washed over for even thinking it when Allie was in such abject misery.

Lindy backed out of the room and let Allie and her friends have some privacy. With a heavy heart, she headed back to the dining room for a bottle of water. She'd already sucked down a glass of champagne without thinking, and though a second glass was tempting right about now, she decided to refrain—just in case she did happen to be carrying Drew's child.

The thought nearly floored her.

The doorbell rang. Lindy fought to get her emotions under check before answering it. Hannah stood on the porch, her smile hesitant. She'd brought a date, and when Lindy made eye contact with him, a slow burn started at the back of her neck and her heart rate tripled. The pizza delivery guy who'd stolen her bracelet!

Gathering her wits, Lindy motioned them inside. "I'm so glad you made it. Come on in."

"I've been looking forward to it all week, thanks for inviting me. Especially considering

I'm related to the stupidest man on the planet." Hannah stepped into the foyer and shucked her coat.

"Can't argue with you there," Lindy teased. "So is your father coming?"

"No, he decided to stay home tonight, but please don't take it the wrong way. Valentine's Day was my parents wedding anniversary."

"My God, I'm so sorry." Lindy grew even more bummed.

"He's okay, just didn't feel much like celebrating."

"I can't imagine anyone would under those circumstances."

Hannah nodded, then gestured to her date. "I hope you don't mind, but Jimmy asked if he could tag along."

Lindy made brief eye contact with Jimmy and a chill raced up her spine. He kept his coat on, she noticed. No doubt so he could stuff his pockets full of her valuables. "No, of course not." She masked her alarm and gestured toward the dining room. "Go grab yourselves some champagne and something to eat. You can toss your coats on the bed in the room across from the library; I'm pretty sure the hall closet is full."

"Great, thanks. I'm hoping there's some cannoli left." Hannah touched Lindy's arm.

"You look incredible, by the way. Drew's a moron."

Lindy smiled her gratitude. "Thanks. And so do you. Love the sweater, it's quite...glittery."

"A Christmas present from Drew," Hannah admitted with a sheepish grin before striding off in search of cannoli.

Jimmy looked around with open interest as he followed in her wake, making the hairs on the back of Lindy's neck stand up. The guy was shifty, no doubt about it. Lindy made a mental note to speak with Drew about him. She couldn't imagine he'd want his sister dating a thief.

Though Lord only knew when she'd see him again—if ever.

An arm suddenly snaked around her waist, and Lindy nearly jumped out of her Manolos. "Whoa, take it easy," Matt said giving her a reassuring squeeze. "What the hell's got you so wound up?"

Leaning into him, Lindy thanked God for Matt. Her rock. "Remember the night I bought pizza and my bracelet came up missing?"

"I remember. And I forgot to ask, did you ever find it?"

"No. But guess who Hannah brought as her date tonight."

He was quiet for a moment. "I'm going to have to go with the pizza delivery guy."

"Exactly. Matt, I have such a bad feeling about him. Hannah said he'd asked to come along. Isn't that a little odd?"

Matt shrugged. "I don't know if it's odd exactly since this is the most extravagant party Redemption's ever seen. But I'll keep an eye on him if it'll make you feel better."

"It would, thanks."

He gave her one last comforting squeeze. "Now go have some fun, and that's an order. I'm going to snag a few cannoli before they all disappear."

"Better hurry, Hannah's on the same mission."

No sooner had Matt strode off than Mike appeared at her side. "I was hoping I might be able to steal a dance from you."

Lindy hesitated. Though Bernie swore up and down she wasn't interested in the handsome officer, Lindy suspected her new friend was full of it. So...if she looked at from that perspective, Lindy would be doing Bernie a favor, wouldn't she? Maybe a visit from the green-eyed monster was just what the stubborn brunette needed. On the flipside, maybe dancing with Mike would keep Lindy from mooning over Drew for the next few hours; maybe she'd actually enjoy herself for awhile. "I'd love to, thanks."

The DJ had set up in the parlor, the largest room in the old mansion. Several couples were slow dancing to the old classic *When A Man Loves A Woman*. Mike swept her into his arms and suddenly they were swaying to the music. Lindy caught Bernie watching them, her heart-shaped face void of the crooked smile Lindy had become so used to.

"She looks miserable, doesn't she?"

Lindy almost laughed over the hopeful tone in his voice. "Oh, yeah. I'd say she's about ready to scratch my eyes out."

"Good." He must have realized what he said and quickly amended, "I didn't mean 'good' as in...well, you know what I meant, right?"

Now Lindy did laugh, a tinkling of sound that felt wonderful considering the turmoil of her own heart. "I know exactly what you meant, and I'm delighted to be your partner in crime, Officer Donovan."

He grinned, then asked in a near whisper, "Is she still watching?"

"Yeah, though she just set her glass down. Crap, I think she's getting ready to leave."

"I apologize in advance, but you know what they say about desperate times."

With that odd warning, Mike bent her over his arm and laid one on her, slanting his mouth across hers with dramatic flair. Shocked to the tips of her toes, it took Lindy a moment to respond. She placed her hands against his chest to push him away, but before she could, Mike was yanked back so hard Lindy stumbled sideways and fell on her ass. She looked up in time to see Drew draw back his fist and clock Mike in the jaw.

Chapter Twelve

Before Drew c\ould take another swing, Charlie and Matt nearly tackled him to the floor in their effort to restrain him. Son of a bitch! He'd been pining for the woman since the moment he'd left her arms, he'd come back to apologize and put a ring on her finger, only to find her kissing another man?

"You need to calm the hell down," Charlie warned. "You just hit a cop, you moron." Out of the corner of his eye, Drew watched Hannah help Lindy to her feet. His remorse was quickly overshadowed by the insane jealousy surging through his veins. Which only pissed him off more. Jealous? He'd never been jealous a day in his life.

"What the hell's your problem, Porter?" Donovan cursed, testing his jaw.

"You know what my problem is, you asshole," Drew countered, struggling against his friends' constraints. "I'm fine, dammit, let me go!"

Charlie and Matt cautiously released him, but continued to flank his sides, ready to grab him again if necessary. No doubt they were just as shocked as Drew by his passionate explosion.

"What? I was dancing with our hostess, the moment felt right, so I kissed her. What's it to you?"

At that moment, Bernie pushed past them and tore from the room. With a muttered curse, Mike ran after her.

Drew settled his eyes on Lindy, who glared poisoned arrows at him. Damn if she wasn't magnificent in her outrage. Not to mention sexy as hell in that strapless red number. He wanted to toss her over his shoulder caveman style, race upstairs to her room and lock out the world so the night could end the way it was supposed to—the way he'd meant for it to end. With a proposal. The ring box stuffed into his front pocket was an unwelcome reminder of just what an idiot he'd been to think a rich socialite like Melinda Spalding would ever agree to marry a nobody like himself.

Lindy broke eye contact first as she marched off in the same direction as Bernie and Mike. Drew eyeballed Charlie and Matt, who both stood alert, no doubt ready to wrestle him to the ground on a moment's notice. He almost laughed at their watchful vigilance. Not that he blamed them. Drew had always been known as the peacekeeper, as even-tempered as a person could be. But all that had changed the moment Matt's infuriating sister skidded into his life. She'd bulldozed her way through his heart, leaving a path of destruction the likes of which he'd never known. Hell, she'd turned him into a jealous, raving lunatic!

And damn if he didn't want her even more now than he had the night they'd made love.

The night she'd declared how eager she was for the plant to open so she could race back to L.A.

Okay, to be fair, that's not actually what she'd said; just that she was thankful the job was running on time. Possibly he'd overreacted a bit. Hell, he'd been grieving for his mother, worried sick about his father and sister. Not to mention he'd panicked a bit on the emotional front. Having never been in love before, he'd realized that night with complete certainty that he'd fallen head-over-heels with Miss Melinda Spalding.

And the revelation had scared the shit out of him. He'd rushed the hell out of there, which may have left the impression he'd used her for sex.

Then he'd spent an extra week in Michigan with his grandparents after his mother's funeral, and had his father slap an 'On Vacation' sign on the front door of the garage. It had been his grandmother who'd talked some sense into him, reminding him of how precious life was and how short it could be. She'd given him the courage to come home and take a chance on love.

Too bad Hot Stuff decided to move on the first chance she got.

"Well? Aren't you going to go after her?" Matt demanded.

"Why should I? She made her choice pretty clear."

"Idiot. Mike's in love with Bernie, has been since high school. He was trying to make her jealous, any fool could see that."

"Maybe not any fool," Charlie countered.

Hope blossomed in Drew's chest. "Then why didn't the jerk-off just ask her out and keep his lips off my girl?"

Matt grinned. "*Your* girl? If the way Lindy just looked at you is any indication, you've got your work cut out for you."

Drew propped his hands on his hips and blew out a hard breath. "I really screwed up, didn't I?"

"Hell," Charlie chimed in, "you've been screwing up with women since you spilled chocolate milk down the front of Tracey Hillman's new white dress in the third grade."

"You just have to bring that shit up, don't you?"

Charlie laughed. "And in sixth grade you hid a garter snake in Lisa Nutter's backpack."

"Yeah, well, I'd like to think I've evolved since then."

"Maybe a little." Charlie gave Drew a thump on the back. "My advice? Go find her and apologize. Might be a good idea to toss an 'I'm sorry' at Mike, too."

"Donovan can kiss my ass." As Drew strode off in search of Lindy, he heard Charlie mutter "Moron".

He found Lindy in the kitchen speaking with Nino. She gave a few quiet instructions, then breezed right past Drew as if he were invisible. A reluctant smile tugged at his lips. Hot Stuff was plenty pissed at him. Undaunted, he pursued her, determined to have it out. And apologize, though maybe not in that order. He certainly owed her that much. If not for tonight, then definitely for avoiding her for the last week and a half. For letting her think the worst when the simple truth was he'd fallen madly in love with the infuriating woman.

She surprised him by grabbing her coat and slipping out onto the back porch. Drew hadn't shed his jacket yet, so he followed her outside. She grasped the railing and gazed off into the glistening, snow-covered forest. Snow that wasn't supposed to have arrived until the wee hours of the night—when he and Lindy would've been snuggled together under her fancy down comforter if things had worked out the way they were supposed to. He watched the twirling flakes come down as he tried to figure out just the right words to say to make her understand.

"Can we please talk?"

"I have nothing to say to you." She didn't so much as look at him.

"That's okay because I have plenty to say to you."

"Unless you want assault charges filed against you, maybe it's Officer Donovan you should be speaking to."

Drew stuffed his hands into his pockets and hunched his shoulder. "I'll square things with Mike later. My only concern right now is you.

I'm so sorry you got caught in the middle when I grabbed Mike. I never meant for you to get hurt."

Lindy crossed her arms and gave a delicate shiver. Drew stepped forward and grasped her shoulders, pressing himself against her to share his warmth. She flinched, but didn't move away. Which was something, he supposed.

"I'm fine. Just fell on my butt. I seem to do that a lot in this town."

He laid a gentle hand against her bruised backside, but she shrugged away with a whispered, "Don't."

He huffed out a sigh of frustration. "Look, I screwed up and I know it. I'm truly sorry about the other night. I had a lot on my mind and…I wasn't thinking straight. Just give me a chance to make it up to you."

"Why?" She stepped away, but finally spun around to look him in the eye. "Because you have an itch you want scratched and I'm convenient?"

Christ, he'd never known a more exasperating woman! "If scratching an itch was all I wanted, I could find plenty of willing women."

"There's that ego I know and despise. So go, find some other 'willing women' and leave me the hell alone."

"Dammit, Lindy, I only want *you*. Why are you giving me such a hard time?"

The wind picked up as the snow began to fall in earnest. Huge flakes swirled around them, and Lindy gave him one last considering look before stepping past him to head back inside. Over her shoulder, she said, "I'd like you to leave now. Please."

She slid the patio door closed behind her, leaving Drew staring after her in mounting frustration. Okay, fine. She needed some time to get over her anger. Drew understood that. He'd needed exactly the same thing after she'd informed him she had every intention of leaving Redemption—and him—once the plant was operating.

Deciding the best thing to do for both of them was to give her some space, Drew hopped over the porch railing and headed home.

The party lost steam and wound down quickly after the Drew fiasco. By 11:00 p.m. everybody had gone home, except Matt and Carrie. Wanting nothing more than to do a little reading in a nice bubble bath, Lindy promised them she'd be fine.

"Are you sure?" Matt asked as he hugged her tight. "I can stay."

"No, please, I'm fine. Just tired. I'm going to take a hot bath, then sleep till noon."

Matt released her with a kiss on the forehead. "Fine. But call me as soon as you wake up."

Lindy shared an eye-roll with Carrie over Matt's zealously protective nature. "Yes, *dad*."

She shut and locked the door behind them with a sigh of relief. Though she loved her brother dearly, all she wanted tonight was to be left alone.

Twenty minutes later, Lindy eased down into a steaming bubble bath, several vanilla-scented candles illuminating the small room with their calming, iridescent glow. She'd grabbed an open bottle of champagne and a glass on her way upstairs, and as she sipped the sparkling liquid, she looked up through the skylight and watched the snow whirl above her.

She'd always loved the snow, had looked forward to the many ski trips her family had gone on when she and Matt were kids—and still did when time permitted, though not for the past few years. On their last trip, Dad and Matt had spent most of their time researching a new company they planned to acquire. Which was the same time she'd started penning her first manuscript. She'd imagined a beautiful countess staring off into the snow-covered countryside anticipating the arrival of her true love, the father of the child she'd just discovered she was carrying.

Damn.

Lindy's hand settled atop her flat stomach. With a disgusted sigh, she set the glass of bubbly aside and reached for the book she'd left on the floor beside the tub.

A loud thump had her sitting up in a rush, heart pounding in her ears. The sound had definitely come from inside the house. She glanced at Bianca, whose own ears had perked up. The pounding became full-blown panic when Bianca took off to investigate.

A sharp, feline hiss followed by a dull thud sent a chill up her spine. Bianca! Lindy bit the inside of her cheek, wanting to call out to her precious baby, but too petrified to utter a sound. Instead, she slid from the tub, blew out the candles, and slipped her robe off the hook on the back of the door with trembling fingers. All she could hear over the roaring in her ears was the howling wind outside as the blizzard arrived in full force. No electrical hum, no knocking of the furnace. Whoever had broken into her house must have cut off the power.

Biting her lip, terrified to make even the tiniest sound, Lindy slowly cracked the door open to peer into her nearly black bedroom. She watched intently for moving shadows, but nothing stirred or shifted. A sitting duck in the bathroom, she crept out into the bedroom and positioned herself behind the door, which she'd left slightly ajar. Nothing but absolute silence. And thanks to the storm, not even a flicker of moonlight filtered in through the window in the hall. She'd just started to convince herself she'd imagined the whole thing when someone sneezed so close to where she stood Lindy swore she felt the spray. Tears sprang to her eyes, and she quickly clamped a hand over her mouth.

"Goddamn, I told you to be quiet!" came a furious whisper from just outside her door.

"I can't help it. I'm allergic to fuckin' cats."

Numb with fear, Lindy somehow forced her legs to move. She inched back away from the door and looked around in a blind panic for someplace to hide. Dropping to her belly, she crawled under her bed just as the door to her bedroom flew open and slammed against the wall.

"Come on out, rich girl," one of them prompted with obvious impatience. "We know you're in here."

Her breath caught as she realized the voice sounded oddly familiar, but for the life of her she couldn't place it. Hell, he could be anyone—someone from the coffee shop, or the grocery store, or the diner. She squeezed her eyes shut and strained to listen as they rummaged through her room, chucking stuff around, slamming dresser drawers, checking the closet and the bathroom. One of them bumped into her dresser and cursed a blue streak.

"Dammit, where the hell is she?"

"She was here; you can still smell the candles. Probably slipped downstairs. Let's go."

"Why did you have to pick such a big goddamn house? Shit, she could be any-goddamn-where."

"Hey, you're the genius who forgot to make sure the fucking flashlight worked before cutting the power."

Their voices grew faint as they hurried down the stairs. Lindy slid out from under the bed and grabbed her purse off the dresser. Cell phone, cell phone...where the hell was her cell phone? With a silent sob, she dumped her purse on the bed, but her phone wasn't there. Then she remembered...she'd set it on the counter in the kitchen!

Okay, calm down. Think.

The landline! She almost laughed aloud at the absurdity of forgetting to check the landline. But when she picked up the receiver, the line was dead. Fear skittered up her spine like icy cold fingers. Looked like she had no choice but to sneak downstairs. Reaching the kitchen undetected would be difficult considering the only way to get there was down the staircase, but she had to try. She could wait and hope they left once they got what they wanted.

But what if *she* was what they wanted? Why else would they be searching for her? If they meant to simply rob her, wouldn't they have simply waited for a day she wasn't home?

Fresh tears filled her eyes and she quickly swiped them away. *Drew*. If only she hadn't been so damn stubborn and had simply let the man apologize, he'd be here right now and...and he'd be in danger, too.

Lindy could hear the intruders rummaging around downstairs, either looking for valuables, for her, or both. Careful not to make a sound, she slipped from her room and crept to the top of the staircase. Taking a deep breath, she padded barefoot down the stairs in a half-crouch, heaving a soundless sigh of relief when she reached the bottom undetected.

A crash of thunder rocked the house. Lindy shrieked, then quickly clamped a hand over her mouth. Dear God, she'd very likely just given away her location! She waited what seemed like an eternity before forcing herself to continue.

Creeping along the wall, careful to stay hidden in the shadows, Lindy reached the kitchen without incident. She slipped inside and cautiously made her way to the center island. Her hand closed over her phone just as someone seized her by the hair and yanked her backward.

"I got 'er, man! She's in the kitchen!"

Survival mode kicked in. Lindy jabbed an elbow back with all her might, nailing the guy in the stomach. He released his hold on her with a muttered curse and she tore out of there, racing back to the staircase, desperate to find another hiding spot. She'd only made it up three steps when they caught her and dragged her into the foyer. She realized they both wore ski masks, so even if she managed to survive the attack, she wouldn't be able to identify them.

They shoved her to the cold tile floor as Lindy kicked and screamed for her life. But they were much stronger than her and had her pinned down in no time. One held her by the ankles while the other held her arms over her head. When she let out another ear-shattering scream, the latter gathered both her hands in one of his and slapped a hand over her mouth so hard her skull cracked against the tile.

"Feisty as hell, ain't she?" said the one holding her ankles, the glee in his tone turning her stomach. He maneuvered until he straddled her knees, then clicked on a flashlight and shined it in her face, momentarily blinding her. "Found this in one of the kitchen drawers."

"I think we're gonna have us a good time here," the other agreed, his sadistic tone chilling the blood in her veins. "Flash that light on her tits, will ya?" He removed his hand from her mouth and yanked open her robe. "Damn," he murmured with near reverence, running one of his disgusting hands over her breasts, pinching cruelly at her nipples. "Nice, rich girl. Very nice."

Lindy fought in earnest, screaming until she thought her lungs would burst. Humiliation burned in her gut and she grew numb with fear, the inevitability of her fate the only fuel she had left to drive her to fight. The scumbag holding the flashlight set it down to pry her legs apart as his cohort knelt on her shoulders and reached for the zipper of his fly.

The front door burst open with such force both men yelped as they lurched backward and stumbled to their feet. Someone rushed in.

"Lindy!"

Drew? Her throat was so raw from screaming she couldn't even say his name, but she could have cried in relief when the beam of the flashlight cut across his handsome face. He'd come back! She sat up in a rush and tried to stand, but one of her attackers grabbed her hair and yanked her to her feet. When he pressed a knife against her throat, Drew stopped dead in his tracks.

"One more step and I'll slit her fuckin' throat." Her captor's wrist flexed and the blade nicked her skin. He'd purposely deepened his voice, she realized, and wondered if it was because Drew might recognize it as well.

Lindy held deathly still, aware of the blood trickling down her neck. Her heart hammered triple time as she waited for Drew to respond.

With surprising calm, Drew said, "You're a dead man."

"Such a hero," her attacker sneered as he slowly backed up, dragging her with him. Lindy took a misstep and the knife bit into her throat again. A whimper escaped her. Suddenly, he shoved her so hard she stumbled into the staircase post and cracked her head.

Lindy's knees gave out as everything went black.

Chapter Thirteen

Drew paced outside the ER as he waited for news on Lindy's condition. She'd still been unconscious when they'd reached the hospital, and so far there'd been no word. He'd called an ambulance immediately, but because he'd chosen to stay with Lindy instead of give chase, her attackers had escaped. One day, Drew swore, he'd make those bastards pay for hurting the woman he loved.

"Drew!"

He spun around in relief at the sound of Matt's voice. Lindy's brother strode toward him, Carrie and Hannah flanking his sides. Hannah rushed forward and threw herself into Drew's arms with a soft sob. On the brink of tears himself, and in desperate need of comfort, Drew held her tight.

"Is she okay?"

"I don't know. She was still unconscious when we got here, and nobody's told me a goddamn thing."

Matt gave him a thump on the back. "It's only been maybe twenty minutes since you called, and Lindy's a lot tougher than she looks, trust me on that."

Carrie gazed up at Matt, love and support shining in her eyes. He gave her shoulder a squeeze before leading her over to the waiting area. Drew and Hannah joined them, but as soon as they sat, Charlie strode out the ER doors and headed their way. Drew swallowed hard, sending up a silent prayer that Lindy's injuries weren't serious or life-threatening.

"Lindy's awake and doing remarkably well considering how hard she hit her head," Charlie informed them. "She has a mild concussion, but that's to be expected."

Relief expelled from Drew's chest with a mighty whoosh. *Thank God.*

"Can we see her?" Matt asked.

"Absolutely. Come on." With a wave of his hand, Charlie led them through the double doors.

They piled into her cubicle, and Drew's heart wrenched when he saw her. A bandage covered her forehead, another wrapped around her throat, and tears stained her cheeks, but to him she had never looked more beautiful.

Matt leaned over to kiss her forehead, but she wrapped her arms around him and pulled him down with a cry of relief. "I've never been so scared in my life," she whispered, though everyone heard her heartbreaking admission.

Drew silently vowed those two rapist sons of bitches would pay dearly for what they did—and tried to do—to Lindy. They may have gotten away for now, but if it was the last thing he did, he'd castrate the both of 'em.

Miss Melinda Spalding had taken up residence in every corner of his heart, and when he'd heard her scream....dear God. To echo what she'd just said, he'd never been so scared in his life. He needed to quit thinking about it or he'd lose his damn mind.

"Me, too," Matt whispered back.

"Bianca?"

Matt looked to Drew, who smiled reassuringly. "She's fine. Tough as nails, just like her mommy."

"Thank God," she murmured, reaching up to finger her bandage.

Matt straightened and stepped back to allow Carrie in. Carrie grasped Lindy's hand, and the two women who'd started off as wary acquaintances, but had become good friends, shared a moment.

Lindy finally made eye contact with Drew. Fresh tears welled in her eyes as she gazed him, so many unspoken words between them.

Matt cleared his throat. "Uh, ladies, I think we need to give these two some privacy."

Carrie released Lindy's hand and stepped back into Matt's embrace. Hannah smiled and gave Lindy's hand a squeeze before following Matt and Carrie from the room.

They stared at each other for a moment.

"I'd never have forgiven myself if those scumbags had..." The words escaped Drew's lips before he could call them back.

"But they didn't. Thanks to you."

"I never should've left," he countered. "I swear, first thing tomorrow I'm having a state-of-the-art security system installed in your house."

"I ordered you to leave, Drew. In no way is any of this your fault. I'm just so grateful you came back." Her voice cracked on the last word, and Drew rushed forward to crush her in his arms.

"I needed you," he admitted in a near whisper, eyes burning. "I couldn't imagine spending another night without you. My damn pride had already kept me away for over a week."

"Why...why did you leave?"

Drew released her from his death grip and reached back to pull one of the chairs up next to the bed. He grasped her hand, kissing her palm before replying. "I realized for the first time in my life, it'd happened. I'd fallen in love. But I knew once the plant was up and running..." Unable to finish, he shrugged.

Lindy searched his face and whispered, "You thought I'd leave you?"

"It wasn't exactly a secret you planned to head home to L.A. as soon as the job was done."

She was quiet for a moment, then asked, "You've heard the expression *Home Is Where the Heart Is*, right?"

"Of course, why?"

"Because I love you, too," she told him, her heart shining in her eyes. A slow grin curved her lips. "Even though you're the most impossibly arrogant man I've ever had the misfortune to know."

Drew tipped his head back and laughed. "I never thought I'd say this, Hot Stuff, but I think we're damn near perfect for each other."

"And I never thought I'd say this, but..." She cast him a coy look through her lashes. "You're right, *Lou*."

Epilogue

"*And* who would you like me to make it out to?" Lindy asked, pen poised over the dedication page of her latest release, *Moonlit Encounter*. She looked up and met Lauren's sheepish smile. Caleb stood grinning beside her, Emma tucked in his arms.

"Me, please." As if in awe, Lauren glanced slowly around, taking it all in—the posters, the stacks of books, the mob of people crammed into the interior of *Coffee To Chai For*, with a line literally spilling out the door.

Lindy was plenty awed herself.

"I just still can't believe it. You're Katelynn Meadows. How crazy is that?"

"How come that doesn't exactly sound like a compliment?" Lindy teased as she signed the book. "I can't imagine why my being a romance author is such a shock to everyone."

Lindy heard a few muffled snickers, but they only brought a smile to her face. Blissfully happy, she tucked a bookmark into the copy she'd just signed and handed it to Lauren, who beamed as if Lindy had just placed a rainbow in her hand. Lindy glanced up at Emma who was busy sucking down one of Carrie's delicious triple berry smoothies. "Hey, sweetie, that sure looks good."

Emma gazed down at her, those little lips working the straw like a siphon. Suddenly she stopped and graced Lindy with the most heart-stopping smile. Lindy's heart melted into a gooey puddle. Gripped by emotions completely new to her, she smiled back. Emma waved as Lauren thanked her and headed off with her prize.

Humbled by the number of people who'd shown up for her first ever appearance as Katelynn Meadows, Lindy signed book after book, chatting with everyone from Allie and Rick, to Motormouth Marv, to Mrs. Steagle from the Piggly Wiggly. The residents of this town had welcomed her into their fold without hesitation, just as they had Matt last summer. They'd made her feel like she belonged, though it wasn't that long ago she couldn't imagine calling this small town home. She'd put her nose in the air from day one, and now she couldn't even fathom living anywhere else. Home truly is where the heart is. And Lindy's heart—and future—were right here in Redemption.

The main reason for Lindy's total euphoria strolled through the door. He stopped, propped his hands on his hips, and gave his head a bemused shake, taking it all in. When those gorgeous baby blues landed on her, Lindy's heart lit up like a bonfire. She loved this man, wholly, completely, and forever.

Good Lord, she sounded like a huge cheeseball!

Drew strode forward, people stepping aside so he could pass. He reached the table and gave her a sexy wink. "Your knight in shining armor reporting for duty. So how's my little author doing?"

She stuck a bookmark in the book she'd just signed and handed it to Mrs. Steagle. "You do know how patronizing that sounded, right?" She softened the comment with a wink of her own.

"Sorry." He cleared his throat and did another sweep of the place. "I was thinking I'd take you out for lunch, but from the look of things, you're gonna be here for awhile."

"Another couple of hours at least. How about dinner? I have a taste for one of Nino's meatball subs."

He quirked a brow. "Really? I've never seen you eat a meatball."

"Probably because I don't like them."

He chuckled. "Hot Stuff, you're definitely gonna keep me on my toes."

Lindy signed one book after another, chatting and laughing with everyone, more at ease with these people than she'd ever been with her friends back in L.A. Drew stood beside her, watching in silence, and she couldn't help but wonder what was going through his mind.

"So, no more thoughts of running home to LA?"

Okay, now that was just scary. They were already finishing each other's thoughts. "I *am* home. I'm exactly where I want to be."

"Glad to hear it." He placed a hand on the back of the chair and leaned down to murmur, "I could eat you with a spoon."

She craned her neck to meet his gaze. Mischief danced in his eyes. "Well then, maybe we should get that Nino's to go," she suggested.

"Sounds like a plan to me."

"I also think we'd better kick start our wedding plans."

"Not that I'm complaining, but is there a particular reason we need to rush?"

Lindy slipped her hand beneath the table and laid it across her tummy. A feeling of pure joy and contentment washed over her, nearly stealing her breath. She'd taken the test just that morning, though she'd known intuitively for weeks.

"I'd like to be able to fit into my wedding dress."

She chanced a glance up at him as her words sank in. His puzzled frown was quickly replaced by open-mouthed shock. He swallowed, squatted down beside her and whispered, "Are you sure?"

Throat thick with emotion, she somehow managed an affirmative nod. Drew's eyes filled with happiness, and at that moment, Lindy could see their future stretched out before them, bright, beautiful, full of good times, plenty of fireworks, but most of all love.

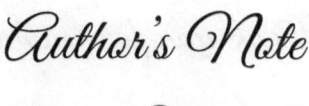

Author's Note

I hope Drew and Lindy's, and Bo and Bianca's, journeys both touched your heart and tickled your funny bone. Stacey Joy Netzel and I would love for you to read the rest of the series and fall in love with the characters who've become our friends.

— *Donna Marie Rogers*

Thank you for reading!

If you enjoyed *Home Is Where the Heart Is*, don't forget to leave a review.

Visit Donna's website to sign up for her newsletter for announcements of all New Releases and *exclusive* sales and content!

www.DonnaMarieRogers.com

Up next in the WELCOME TO REDEMPTION series

The Heart of the Matter

Welcome to Redemption Series
Book 6

STACEY JOY NETZEL

All Allie Daniels ever wanted was a family of her own—until her doctor informs her she'll never be able to have children. She hides her desolation, refusing to let any man close enough to see her broken heart. Most certainly not the town veterinarian, whose cute three-year-old son reminds her of what she'll never have.

Rick Wilde had a serious crush on Allie back in high school, but life took them in different directions. Now a single parent, he returns to Redemption several years later to raise his son, Lukas. His interest in Allie is renewed, but her shoulder is colder than the bitter winter wind.

Brought together by an orphaned kitten, Allie finds herself helpless to resist Lukas's impish innocence—not to mention Rick's warm charm and sexy good looks. Does she dare take a chance on an impossible dream, or will Rick's desire for more kids devastate their future?

Excerpt

*A*llie hung up her jacket and rubbed her arms while waiting for Rick to exit the bathroom. The sooner he left, the sooner she could forget about the whole night and go back to avoiding him. It was always hard to see him, but at least she could be thankful he hadn't had his beautiful little boy with him. Lukas looked exactly as she'd have pictured Rick at that age. Same dark hair and brown eyes and adorable as could be.

Anytime she saw them around town her heart constricted, making it hard to breathe as she hurried in the opposite direction. And the few times she hadn't been able to force herself to leave right away, she saw how attentive he was to his perpetually-smiling son. He seemed like such a good dad.

Footsteps sounded on the hardwood floor. She straightened and shook off the longing, heart-warming, painful thoughts. She was still mad at him. *Easy lay*. She should've smacked him for that crack.

He hesitated when he saw her still standing by the door. She hated that she noticed his hair looked black from the moisture of the melted snow. And Lord, was he tall up close. He stopped a few feet in front of her. She reached blindly for the door handle while trying to tear her gaze from eyes the color of the most decadent dark chocolate she could imagine.

He took another step closer and leaned forward. She shrank back while her heart beat a crazy rhythm in her chest. His warm hand closed over her cold one on the door knob, preventing her from opening it. A tingle worked its way up her arm even after she pulled away from his touch.

"I apologize for what I said earlier."

Her stomach fluttered as his husky, baritone voice flowed over her. It took a second for his words to register, but the moment they did, she snapped back to reality.

"Just because I date a lot does not mean I sleep around."

His gaze shifted away, along with his body. "I didn't mean to imply that you did."

"You did more than imply."

"The words came out wrong."

"And sometimes what a person actually thinks just pops right out."

"No," he denied, his jaw tight. "I was referring to the jerk you were with."

"You don't even know him," she retorted. That she was sure of because she'd met Brent in her web-design class in Green Bay at the technical college last semester. Although with the way the evening had progressed, and after what Brent had said, she knew Rick was right about him, darn it.

"I know his kind."

"Recognized a kindred spirit, is that it?"

His brows drew together. "That's the second time you've said that and yet I haven't done anything to you. What's your problem with me?"

You've turned into a nice, responsible guy, you're too good-looking, and you have what I want most and can never have.

Allie scoffed and raised her chin despite the sting of tears that threatened with the last thought. "As if you don't know."

He lifted his hands. "I really don't. Since I came home two years ago you've barely said two words to me."

"That's because back in high school you were a jerk."

His frown deepened. "I was?"

"You teased me every chance you got," she accused. "Got all your party-animal jock buddies in on the act, too. In fact, you did such a good job that after you graduated, I still had three more years of that crap with the rest of the football team."

"That was high school."

"It was mean." Allie bit her lip. Rick had never been as bad as the other guys...but maybe that was because he was the only one she pretended to laugh off?

"Seriously?" he asked after a long moment, his brows arched. "That's why you avoid me— why you walk the other direction when you see me at the grocery store or on the sidewalk? Because you think I was mean to you back when we were in high school, over *fifteen years* ago?"

She glanced away. Sounded petty and absurd to her too, but it wasn't like she could tell him the real reason why, so she kept her mouth shut.

"You want to know why I acted like that back then?"

The low question made her stomach lurch and brought her gaze back to his. Her heart started racing again, especially when he crowded her in the corner, darkening it with his shadow.

"Even as a freshman, you were the smartest person I knew. You were in all the college classes with me and got better grades than I did. Every time I opened my mouth around you, nothing came out right, and you'd give me this...*look*, and I felt stupid. Not the most mature way to handle it, but there you have it."

Allie fought to keep her mouth from hanging open in surprise. She'd had no clue. In fact she'd always felt stupid around *him*.

He leaned closer. Palms and back flattened against the wall, she stared at his chest, unable to say a single word. Besides, if she looked up, she'd see his mouth so close to hers and want to rise on her tiptoes. He'd been drinking beer earlier, but now he smelled winter fresh.

He braced one hand against the wall beside her head. The other he tunneled through her hair to cup the back of her head while his thumb tipped her chin up. Her heart banged into her ribs. *Gum.* He'd been chewing gum in the truck. She swallowed as if a piece were stuck in her own throat when his gaze locked with hers.

"And then there's this. I've wanted to do this since the day you corrected Mr. Counsell's equation in advanced chem the second week of class."

She'd guessed he was going to kiss her, but, *Oh, my, God, Rick Wilde was kissing her!*

The Heart of the Matter is available now at your favorite bookstore or online retailer.

About the Author

USA Today Bestselling author Donna Marie Rogers inherited her love of romance from her mother. Romance novels, soap operas, *Little House on the Prairie*—her mother loved them all. And though it wasn't until years later Donna would come to understand her mother's fascination with Charles Ingalls, Donna's love of the romance genre is every bit as all-consuming.

A Chicago native, Donna now lives in beautiful Northeast Wisconsin with her husband and children. She's an avid gardener and home-canner, as well as an admitted Halloween fanatic. Her passion to read is only exceeded by her passion to write, so when she's not doing the wife and mother thing, you can usually find her sitting at the computer, creating exciting, memorable characters, fresh new worlds, and always happily-ever-afters.

www.DonnaMarieRogers.com